The Case of Mothy

Rhiannon D. Elton

The Case of Mothy © Rhiannon D. Elton 2020
The Wolflock Cases: Book 2
Second edition

First Edition published January 2017
Second Edition published March 2020

ISBN: 978-0-6487636-2-8 (paperback)

info@rhiannoneltonauthor.com

Cover compiled by Rhiannon D. Elton

This is a work of fiction. Names, characters, places, and incidents either are the products of the author's imagination or are used fictitiously. Any resemblance to actual persons, living or dead, businesses, companies, events, or locales is entirely coincidental.

Cataloguing-in-Publication information for this title is listed with the National Library of Australia.

Published in Australia by Rhiannon D. Elton and Pelaia Adventures

Declaration of Intention

Merry meet,

The purpose of the books the author writes is to give representation to as many peoples, creatures and landscapes as they can. Although written from the perspective of a Caucasian teenage boy, the author hopes to offer a light into the harmony of different cultures and creeds of people. The author's aim is to promote harmony, understanding and compassion in all areas, while also inspiring readers to stand up against injustice and be critical thinkers in life.

While the author does their best to research, interview and highlight the best parts of people, they are only human and can make mistakes. The author asks you gently educate them by sending them an email in order to discuss anything that may have caused harm to a group of people unintentionally.

The author believes that the cure for ignorance is education, but please approach the topic cordially in order to avoid any knee-jerk cognitive dissonance.

Finally, the viewpoints displayed in the books comes from a particular character and is not necessarily that of the author's. The author seeks to display flaws, growth and human nature on many levels, and hopes that you will analyse the character of the protagonist without adopting any negative behaviours from them.

Merry part, and merry meet again.

Mystentine University

Mystentine City

Hiwrfóa Forest

Vaggafel Forest

Wourst

Creast

Iirid

Shorsh

Hatfjorn Lake

Dragon's Spine Mountain Range

Vorör Pass

Lelughwin Forest

Krieger Zwerg Keep

Forestria

Zilber River

Woods of Dunkelheit

Plugh

0   100

Seebruecke Dock

Scale in Miles

Woods of Veil

(c) 2018 Rhiannon D. Elton

CHAPTER 1

Write Answers, Wrong Questions

Wolflock leaned on the smooth grey taffrail, scoffing and rapping his long fingers irritably as the breeze fluttered the letter clenched in his left fist. He'd thought it was an acceptable time to write to his little sister, Myna, detailing the events of the last week but he wasn't yet satisfied with the letter's contents. It had already been a dismally long seven days on the Silver Ice Hair and, so far, he had minimal time to himself to do anything of true enjoyment. Apparently, when aboard the vessel, the captain required all the company to take part in activities. These included all manner of foolish social events through the day like ball games, novel and history readings, evening dances and deck picnic lunches. Initially, the promise of seeing the ships' specimens in varying dynamics gave Wolflock a newfound excitement, but it only took an evening for him to realise the crew and company were primarily average in all areas of life. The blanket of frustrating boredom shrouded him once more.

"I should never have looked for that snuffle..." he bemoaned as he watched waves crash on the grassy banks in the ship's wake. *I could have continued to sneak out with Mothy's assistance and be free of these tiresome bonding activities...*

The edges of the dark blue river became increasingly mottled with autumn leaves, redressing the earth in her new gown as the sleepy pink twilight lingered longer during each dawn and dusk. The very earth itself seemed to struggle to wake in the morning and crave an early night's rest as the days grew colder.

A flash of movement caught his eye to the left, and he stood bolt upright, trying to glimpse the source. *Nothing... must have been another fish...*

He had been waiting to see the maramuti creatures Grogen had spoken about, which remained the only reason he was outside and risking another social ambush calling him to some other mundane engagement. He wouldn't have minded Mothy's company, as he got along with the lad very well, but there was no one else on the ship was of any interest to him. Mothy wasn't educated in many academic schools of thought, but he had a refreshing perspective on life. He'd travelled a bit while he was younger, and he told Wolflock he'd gotten a short education in mining, blacksmithing, carpentering, farming and tailoring. Everything practical and trade worthy had at least been touched upon in his life, giving him a curious insight that Wolflock had fed off for many hours of entertainment. There was no reason to distrust his word as he didn't appear to try to show off his skills, but rather just seemed excited to share his knowledge. He had unknowingly presented himself as so naïve and genuine that Wolflock had no desire to deny his company. It also helped that Mothy hung off every word Wolflock spoke, which was a pleasant change from the constant dismissal he received from the older passengers.

He sighed and watched as pale-barked maple trees trickled their leaves into the river that lashed against their roots. Behind the dining hall was one of the few places people didn't venture too often. Wolflock had felt that he could get some peace and quiet, but even in the serenity of the autumnal landscape before him he couldn't silence the chatter in his mind.

Had his father recovered from the political drama in Plugh? What was Myna studying today? Was she tutoring Ginia? Had they done what he said and fed the good apples to the horses? How was Brennan, his horse?

He wanted a way to contact home besides the letter in his hand that he wouldn't be able to post until they reached Irid in over a month. His heavy chest heaved a sigh as he realised that he didn't want to be alone, but he didn't want to be with any of the passengers. He wanted to be with his family. He just didn't want to be in Plugh.

Wolflock continued to wallow miserably as he gazed out, catching another tiny splash from an excited fish catching insects. The scent of bread being baked in the oven from the kitchen just behind him began to creep over his shoulder. He found it difficult to pretend he was in solitude as the song hummed by the days chef in the kitchen came through clearly. Judging by the gruffness and the style of song it was Goden's job today. The longer he waited for the song to pass and his silence to resume, the more the chatter of the passengers grew as they settled on their picnic blankets for a sunny deck lunch. The sound wafted around the dining hall on the wind like an irritating bug that aimed directly for his ears.

His sulking didn't last for much longer though as Mothy bounced around the corner with a smile as bright as the midday sun.

"Merry meet, Lockie," he chimed.

To his knowledge, Wolflock had never had a pet name before and he wasn't yet sure if he enjoyed being called 'Lockie' or not. He hadn't protested because, although it was new to him to not be addressed as "Mr Felen" or "Master Felen", it wasn't entirely unpleasant. He also felt the need to have someone to talk to on the ship who at least appreciated his conversation. On top of all his other reasons for liking Mothy, he liked that he admired Wolflock for his most prized quality. His wit.

"Merry meet, Mothy," he sighed and folded his letter away in his trouser pocket.

"Are you still being grumpy?" The blond boy smirked and mirrored his position against the railing.

"I'm sure I don't know what you mean," Wolflock sniffed indignantly.

Mothy drew a long, deliberate breath in and exhaled as if he'd just smelt the best baked goods in the world.

"Isn't this incredible?" He slapped his hands on

the banister. "I mean, just look at that! We're on a ship heading to another country. We get this amazing view and we get to stay with such fabulous people. We are so very lucky! We don't even have to work!"

Wolflock raised a sharp black eyebrow.

"I fail to see how a change of scenery is lucky. People worked hard to get to this point in their lives. I don't believe that luck had much to do with it."

Chuckling and shaking his head, Mothy closed his eyes and listened to the wind and water for another deep breath. "You know you have to stop being so grumpy. You're not making any friends being foul about everyone else being allowed out on deck and not just you."

"Well, I was the one who found the snuffle. I'm the one who deserved the reward. They have gotten to share it for the week and now they should descend below deck until they do something of equal use," Wolflock grumbled and crossed his arms. "The least the Captain could have done is asked if I actually wanted to share it. They were all on here for two weeks and did nothing to rectify the situation."

"You should be content that you've brought so much joy to the people here and benefitted the whole ship. Isn't that reward enough?" he asked maternally.

Wolflock felt patronised as Mothy acted as if he were teaching him how to share.

"Well, frankly no!" He raised his nose. "I thought they would be far more interesting company but now it appears that they are just like the Plugian common folk. Now I am just hoping to get peace and quiet-"

"And find a way to get the run of the ship? All the ship for you to make you so much better than the common folk below?" Mothy snorted dryly looking through him with keener eyes than Wolflock had seen from him.

Wolflock fell silent, feeling the sting of being reprimanded. He turned away, pretending to just watch for more maramuti.

Mothy chuckled and stepped closer, bumping his elbow to Wolflock's. Wolflock refused to respond. Mothy wriggled closer and pressed his whole arm against his friend's rolled up white sleeve. Wolflock caught him in his periphery and turned his head sharply away.

Childish... he sniffed, pulling a disgusted face in order to suppress a grin.

Mothy caught it and snickered, pressing his arm even tighter, nearly pushing Wolflock along the banister.

"So... did you want to show me how amazing and

brilliantly learned you are, my duke?"

Wolflock rolled his eyes so hard his whole face moved with them until they locked onto Mothy's glittering bluish grey ones. He had noticed, over the week, that Mothy's eyes changed colour slightly from day to day. Sometimes vibrant sky blue, sometimes aqua and sometimes hints of brown that glinted golden. The only people Wolflock had known to have this phenomenon where Seers, people gifted with the enhanced sixth sense of aura vision, but Mothy had laughed it off and scratched his chin thoughtfully when Wolflock questioned him about it, saying he knew nothing about it.

"I told you not to call me by those titles. If you must know, my father is a Lord. He owns a bit of land that has residents on it. That makes him a Lord. We're not related to the royal family in any clear way. I assure you."

Mothy pulled his head back as if he'd just tasted something dreadfully bitter.

"Well, I certainly won't be calling you that! Anyway, lunch is nearly ready, and I want you to show me how you do your thing."

"My thing?" Wolflock frowned as they began walking to the midship.

"Yeah, yeah! The thing you do when you look like a fortune teller but, really, you're just looking at all the bits of a person that they haven't hidden, which gives away their secrets. I want to know how you do that!"

"Well, my dear Mothy, it is simply the skills of observation and deduction. One must glimpse the little details, know what they mean and then put all the pieces together to make a whole story."

"Sounds easy. Like a puzzle?"

"More or less." Wolflock gave a half nod.

"Well, this will be a good test of your puzzle solving skills. You can tell me about the other passengers, and I'll tell you if you're right. The only people who have been on the ship longer than me are the crew."

Wolflock found the idea intriguing and a small smile crept onto his face. He could once again impress his friend and feel proud of his honed abilities.

As they approached the mid-deck, he saw the same tartan patterned picnic blankets as the crewman, Goden, brought out platters of hard cheeses, vegetables on skewers and cliffberry marmalade sandwiches.

"I can certainly entertain the notion." He sat down across from Mothy on the same blanket as Froderyk, the rude coughing gentleman, his wife, Fuhji, and the

Ulukenic woman Haatji.

"Merry meet," Mothy smiled to the group as he took a sandwich. "Wolflock is going to show us his trick. Perhaps start with... Froderyk and Fuhji."

"What? What's this now?" Froderyk's brow furrowed and his eyes shot around.

"Oh yes! A game! That will be delightful!" Fuhji giggled and laid her hand on her partner's clenched fist.

Wolflock eyed them intently, Fuhji smiling as if she was about to get her palm read and Froderyk glancing about with tight lips.

Wolflock focused and what he picked up on instinctually began to take shape. It was like looking at the pieces of a beautiful beetle for the first time with a magnifying glass. Every leg, hair, and a piece of shell glittered before him and created an image of the whole being.

Fuhji sat with a straight back, prim and proper, her hands delicately laying across whatever she touched. Her eyes had a subtle almond shape and her cheekbones were high on her smooth face. Her boyish short brown hair was showing the slightest signs of new growth and she had occasionally raised her hand to her shoulder as if to feel for something. Her left hand sported the fainter skin where a ring once wrapped around her wedding finger, but her right hand had a fine silver ring with a huge clear, twinkling gemstone in it. Her nails were painted but had grown out and the polish was very good quality judging by the lack of cracks and persistent shimmer.

Froderyk, on the other hand, hunched his shoulders forward and his skin was more weathered than Fuhji's. He'd clearly seen a lot more sun and work than his wife. He sported a detailed silver band on his wedding finger and adorned his neck and wrists with thick gold and silver jewellery. Wolflock spied a glint of an earring under his coarse brown hair before a vein began throbbing in the sour man's temple. His mottled brown eyes, thin lips and overhanging eyebrows gave him a rather doltish appearance, even if he wore fine clothes. His shirt was currently unbuttoned, but Wolflock couldn't mistake the crisp collar and precise cut of his own tailor's family style.

"Stop looking at us!" he snapped.

Wolflock sneered.

"How am I meant to show Mothy what I do if I'm not able to do it? Anyway," he pointedly turned to his friend and waved his hand to dismiss the lesser man. "Fuhji here is one of the daughters of a noble family in

Corl. I assume it is the Korsaki family who immigrated to Corl to sell grains and now control the Quarenth grain farming standards. My aunt Liona often tells us she has tea with them-"

"Are you Quathie's cousin? I used to love her embroidery. It was always the most beautiful at tea," Fuhji chimed with a glowing smile.

Wolflock stopped and blinked at the interruption. "I don't speak much with my family in Corl."

"Oh." Fuhji leaned away and averted her gaze.

"As I was saying, Fuhji has been born amongst the circle accustomed to wealth and refined etiquette training. She was also engaged for many months, most likely to the son of another family who was believed to be of political or social advantage but with whom she had only a passing interest in, if that. Her hair has been shorn off, so she was harder to identify whilst leaving Corl, likely to have made her look like a young man or Froderyk's brother, rather than his wife.

Then there is Froderyk, who apparently came from poor breeding and earned his wealth but would never be considered by one of the better families due to their distaste in new money. His defensive and over-protective nature all come from a place of insecurity, since he knows those he covets the company and appreciation of so intensely will never accept him. Due to this, it's likely that he was raised in the worst parts of Corl, as is shown by the typical thickly set brow and more squared features of his face. He also has a conveniently nasty cough, so I wouldn't spend too much time near him for fear of catching his illness-"

"Hah!" Mothy laughed loudly, but Wolflock could see the strain on his face. "Good one, Lockie! You're such a joker. Take no notice, Froderyk."

A few people from neighbouring blankets had turned to see what the crackle of anxious energy was but turned slowly back to their food when Mothy spoke up. Fuhji began cooing affectionately to her husband, drawing the fiery redness from his face as if her words were cool water.

"Did you just dismiss me?" Wolflock asked incredulously, hurt that his friend would brush him off like that.

"Yes. Were you trying to pick a fight? Because that's how you pick a fight. When I asked you to show me how you used your smarts to figure things out, I didn't mean for you to be mean to anyone." Mothy shook his head apologetically. "Besides, if you're going to aggravate someone, you should probably not do it to someone a head and a half taller than you."

"Brains always beats brawn," Wolflock retorted.

"Not when the brain is in a pampered boy of fifteen Summers and the brawn is a man who had to fight for everything he ever got and worked three jobs."

"I'd like to see him try`

After a long pause, Mothy asked, "You don't speak to many people, do you?"

"I'm sure I don't know what you mean. You asked me to tell you what I saw, and I told you. I did nothing wrong," he shrugged. It was of no consequence to him what Froderyk thought.

"Well... why don't you try to tell me something nice about someone else... What about Dlumi?" Mothy had caught her eye and waved.

Wolflock raised his eyebrow. He knew a few things about Dlumi already. He had walked passed her room a few days ago, noting the typical, if not old-fashioned, business trunk with bands carved with sigils of the goddess of fortune and protection wrapping around it, but it had been left open with only a few items of clothing thrown into it. The case itself was outdated. Most business people these days had more compartments for various items and a separate section for their own belongings. Dlumi frequently wore a gold-plated necklace and a copper bracelet, but both were tarnished, showing their true worth, and lighter patches of skin revealed where she had sold her other jewellery. Her skin was tanned from being in the hot sun of the South, but her broad shoulders and towering height told him she was a native of central Shiriling.

"I see nothing kind about lying for the sake of anyone's feelings. If I can see their secrets, then clearly they are not hiding them well and my evaluation does them a service so they may either come to grips with the reality of the situation or try to hide them more effectively."

Wolflock drew in a breath and began his verbal torrent.

"That being said, Dlumi is an incompetent business woman from Corsh or somewhere nearby, leaving after she fought with her family. And of course, because she comes from central Shiriling, her education has revolved around chopping trees and carving stone, which explains why her business style is antiquated and holds no relevance to how business is performed in more sophisticated areas. Her tarnished jewellery only just hides the lighter skin on which it was previously adorned, telling us that she had to sell the jewellery she wore rather than the wares she meant to sell."

Dlumi let out a choked cry and grasped her wrists, trying to hide her shame, but Wolflock ignored her.

"It's likely that she purchased these items early in her journey but was unable to identify them as being of low quality due to never having handled such things before. She began in Shellinden and was forced to move North in order to try to establish her business after her ineptitude moved her closer and closer to home. Now, with nothing left, she is returning home to beg for more money or skulk back and do whatever her family demands of her. But let's be honest, it probably a safer bet than venturing out again to try her hand at another pipe dream. If she had left with her family's blessing then she would have just been able to write them a letter and not return in person, wasting time and money."

Dlumi's grey eyes became stormy with rage and her bear-like face contorted into a snarl. Mothy's gaze darted back and forth with fear as he moved between Wolflock and the reddening Corshwoman.

"Lockie... Uh... Maybe no more?" he swallowed.

"What? You asked me!" Wolflock protested and

banged his fist into the deck, making Mothy flinch. "It's my turn now. I get to pick someone. This is a grand game! A real kicker!"

Every person's eyes and ears were on Wolflock as he persisted with fervour. He would not be silenced. This would not be Plugh all over again! He would not be pushed around for the sake of others' games.

Smiling smugly his eyes focused in on the Blickland sisters.

"Ah! Look there. Ungul."

The near silent muscular woman with skin like night. She never smiled and was never away from her sister. Silver tattoos wrapped emblazoned flames around her body. Her tightly braided hair made her forehead stretch even further back, giving her a hawkish look. Her black eyes blazed around, burning anyone who appeared even slightly curious about her and her sister's presence.

"Yes, that is her. Good work. Let's get some food-"

But Wolflock couldn't care less.

"You can see by her disagreeable demeanour and taciturn attitude that she has many secrets, none of which she guards particularly well. Again, the education in the Blickland forest folk is primarily survival and not as sophisticated as Shellinmerth or Grothener. She's clearly guarding her sister from escaping again after she fell pregnant to a man who resided in Shellinden, which is where they boarded. The stretch marks on her hips and stomach say that she was pregnant to full term, as does the customary midwife bracelet on her wrist with the infant bead. But the question here is where is the man and the child? The man clearly had no intention of honouring the woman or the child, the stress of which could have caused a miscarriage or stillbirth which is why there is no man, no baby and a sister captive to her family duties. As Blickland folk seldom leave their forest, I can assume your family lives in the southern border which means the man was travelling, which then tells me that this was a sordid affair, not approved by your parents and the man believed it would be a very temporary thing. But what kind of parents don't approve of love affairs? Noble ones. Ungul and Uhnha are the children of a Blickland noble family and to prevent disgrace, Ungul as the eldest child went to drag her sister back come fire or high water! The reason I know that? Because older siblings always get that face of resentment for having to defend their impetuous youngers!"

Wolflock didn't know when he had stood up, but

he found his arms outstretched, his voice growing louder and his tone becoming more commanding. He was putting on a show to shut down anyone who would tell him to be silent ever again.

Finally, he turned back to Mothy, sneering down at him. He had won. He had not been silenced, and he had shown the ship his prowess. None of them could question his intelligence. None of them could tell him he was wrong now.

Mothy looked like a ghost.

His eyes were wide, and he looked terrified. But he wasn't frightened of Wolflock. He looked past him.

Straight at Ungul.

Wolflock turned and saw Ungul rising like a dark dragon. Dlumi, too, rose like a bear, and Froderyk like a pit bull. They had their hungry, raging eyes fixed directly on him and they wanted blood.

"Ah... Lockie..." Mothy gulped and, in one smooth motion, he crouched on his toes. "Run!"

Rhiannon D. Elton

CHAPTER 2

The Failed Test

Wolflock didn't have time to speak before the three brutes charged at him. His body prickled with adrenaline and he ran. He was astounded they would behave in such a manner, but he conceded that he should have expected it from such poorly refined people. Just like in Plugh.

His feet hit the planks of the deck hard as he raced around the back of the ship, wishing he'd hid there all day now. Why had he let Mothy entice him into this stupid game? He should have stayed put and ignored them all like he wanted to. This clearly showed that they weren't worth his time. They were just like everyone else.

He looped around the back of the dining hall, glimpsing blond hair ducking down onto the Captain's balcony below. He could barely take a moment to look as Froderyk had hurled an oar from one of the lifeboats. He ducked down just in time, feeling the oar tear out a few black hairs as it clattered over the railing and into the water below. Wolflock whipped around the side of the dining hall only to see Dlumi had cut him off. She was standing with her arms and legs spread wide, as if she was cutting a young horse's escape from the paddock. Wolflock smirked. He'd seen Brennan do this before. He ran at her and, as she stooped to catch him, he leapt up over her head and sprung off her upper back onto the central mast rigging. He climbed as fast as he could to the crow's nest. Surely, he'd be able to see a way to escape them from there.

Dlumi began climbing, spittle flying from her mouth as she hurled her weight up the ropes. Froderyk and Ungul were close behind her. Just as he swung himself into the crow's nest, he felt a strong hand grab his heel, but they couldn't grasp him tightly enough and he slipped out.

That's when he realised that he'd done the worst

thing he possibly could.

There was no way out from here. He looked around for anything, but it was too late. Ungul was swinging herself over the edge ready to throw him from the large wooden bucket they stood in. Wolflock would not shrink away though. He would not let them tell him he was wrong. Everything he'd said was correct. Everything he'd done was right. He would not be scorned for his wit!

A motion caught his eye to the rear of the ship and he glanced to see Mothy waving urgently at him. Wolflock understood.

He looked down but as Dlumi's massive arm bulged over the side; he saw no way down that he liked.

"You're going to pay for your rudeness, boy!" Dlumi growled, launching forward to tackle him.

Wolflock jumped up and balanced precariously on the edge of the crow's nest. If he waited for them all to be in the one space, he could give himself as much time as he needed to get to Mothy. Ungul was the closest and probably the most adept at climbing as she beat Dlumi to the top even with her head start. Froderyk was easier to outrun and he could dodge Dlumi. He just had to wait for Froderyk to get to the top. He shifted to Dlumi and nearly lost his balance. Finally, his heart hammering in his chest,

Wolflock saw Froderyk's hand appear, followed by a furious yell.

"We've got you now, boy!"

Wolflock's mouth tried to twitch in a smirk as he swallowed his fear. He jumped off the wooden ledge and propelled himself toward the lower back sail. For a second, he felt like he was flying; the wind rippling through his black hair and nothingness surrounding him. He felt a moment of elation when the thick canvas sail cradled him, but the beam beneath was too round and smooth. He couldn't hold on. His grip slipped, and he crashed onto the roof of the dining hall, feeling the wind knocked out of his chest. His whole spine felt jarred and there was a bruised ache on his left thigh, but he pushed through the sensation as he scrambled to his feet. He didn't take a moment to glance back at the three figures starting to race back down after him again. He just ran to the back of the dining hall, leapt down onto a crate he'd noted earlier. He took four strides and stepped up onto the taffrail. Taking a breath and grabbing onto the rail, he jumped off the back of the ship. The air and spray of the river breeze passed him as he swung down onto the balcony below. He felt something grab his trouser leg and pull him faster; the momentum causing them both to topple over into a heap on the floor.

"He's in Captain's quarters! Get him!" Froderyk shouted from above.

Mothy scrambled off Wolflock and dived under the table in the middle of the Captain's room.

"I think they'll find us under there," Wolflock said darkly, rubbing his leg.

"Doubt it," Mothy chuckled and opened the hatch.

"How did you know about this place?" Wolflock grinned as Mothy urged him into the small passage.

"I'll tell you later," he laughed and pushed Wolflock in, following him just as the door crashed open and heavy footsteps trampled into the room.

"He's got to be in here somewhere!" Froderyk snarled, and they heard him ransacking one of the cupboards.

Mothy blinked down at Wolflock, his arms still raised, holding the grate open with a nervous look. Wolflock understood. If he closed the grate, it would make a noise, and they'd hear them, but his arms shook with the weight of the metal.

They listened like nervous hares as the three above looked through the room to no avail, but Ungul's heavy shoeless step came closer and closer to the table. She reached down menacingly, grasping the edge of the silver and white tablecloth and was just about the lift it as a bead of sweat dripped down from Mothy's brow.

"What are you all doing in here!?" Captain Blutro's voice boomed throughout the room. Wolflock caught the grate and helped Mothy ease it down as the Captain drowned out the other noises. There was such authority in his voice that Wolflock wouldn't have believed it was the same sobbing, hysterical man from the week before had he not seen it himself. "Do you think for a moment he'd stay in here? He's probably back in his room! Shame on you all for being so riled up by a young upstart! If any of you lay a hand on the lad, you'll be answering to me. And if you don't put down my underwear, you'll be dragged behind the ship until we reach the ice, Mr Froderyk!"

Both Mothy and Wolflock had to stuff their fists in their mouths to keep from laughing. They heard the three pursuers leave sourly, followed by the Captain's grumble as he tidied his room. Mothy grinned down at Wolflock, his face barely illuminated by the light, making the pristine tablecloth above them glow.

"So... you come here often?" he whispered and raised an eyebrow suggestively.

"I-I do not even know what to say to that!" Wolflock scoffed and shoved him away. "Not as often as you, apparently."

Mothy just smirked and backed out of the tunnel. The lack of awkwardness in his peculiar movements made him look unnatural. As he followed, the thought crossed Wolflock's mind that he might be some kind of strange elf or other worldly being.

I mean... he seems to like me. That has got to mean he is not normal.

"If we slip down to the hull and give them time to cool off, dinner won't feel as terrible. No one wants to eat when someone is glaring at them. There's an empty crate I left snacks in."

"I do not know why they are so upset. I told the truth. They would be more upset if I told lies about them."

"You said unkind things about them. Things they wanted to keep private. It doesn't matter that they aren't untrue, but they are unkind. And you didn't have their permission to discuss those things in front of others. They're embarrassed. For most people, humiliation is worse than torture. Come on. The coast is clear."

Wolflock pursed his lips and looked away. A feeling was creeping into his stomach that made him feel odd and uncomfortable. He'd never really felt guilt before, and he could often justify his actions well enough to not feel bad about them, but Mothy's gentle reprimanding stung him far worse than the irrational anger of the beasts that had chased him.

"Well, if you had not dismissed me the first time, I wouldn't have been spurred on and gotten mad enough to-"

"Are you saying that you are so powerless that another person controls your emotions?"

"Wait-what?"

Mothy barely glanced over his shoulder to rebuke Wolflock with those words, making him feel like someone had slapped him. They descended into the dusty hull to the smell of dry herbs, linen and old hemp rope. Barrels were stacked and neatly labelled against the wall, and the crew kept passenger belongings to the central middle and partitioned off with thinner rope. They positioned crates of tradable goods at the front along with the food and drink, while spare ropes, a second anchor and other equipment for the ship was kept at the back. Mothy guided them to the furthest dark corner and began using a box of matches to light a little candle melted onto a plate. Someone had turned the crate on its side and the lid discarded, leaving it open to the back of the ship.

Wolflock crawled into the crate after Mothy and sat on the blanket inside. Mothy propped himself back on a brown jacket and grabbed a bowl of dried fruit and a pitcher of water, tipping over a female doll made of bound herbs as he did so. Had Tinni put this here?

"Did you set up this place?" Wolflock looked around curiously.

Mothy scratched his head, perplexed. "No. I just found it. I mean... the food is mine. I brought that."

"What did you mean before when you said I was powerless?" Wolflock lifted his nose, pursing his lips.

Mothy chuckled, shaking his head. "My Ma used to tell me that if you say someone made you do something, especially if they made you feel something, that you had given all your power over to them. That you trusted that person more than yourself with your inner peace. If I made you mad, that means either I'm really powerful or you're pretty weak."

"I am not weak!" Wolflock snapped, astounded that Mothy could believe something so preposterous.

"No? No. I suppose not. But you behaved poorly."

"I... they should not have taken offence! By your

logic, they should have not given me such power over their emotions. They're weak for responding the way they did."

"Perhaps. But people are flawed. It's those who learn from their mistakes and misgivings that can resolve their flaws and find greatness."

"You sound like a soothsayer. Where is all this coming from?"

Mothy shrugged. "Do you know what date it is?"

Wolflock thought for a moment. "The fifteenth of Eolas Revari. Why?"

"Autumn makes me a bit tired," Mothy mumbled and scratched his cheek. "Listen, please Lockie. I don't like arguing. I know I upset you when I told the others what you were saying wasn't serious. I was just trying to give you a hint that you'd upset Froderyk. Then you went on a rampage and upset Dlumi and Ungul too. None of them deserved to be spoken to like that. It wasn't polite."

Wolflock turned away, hot, angry tears prickling his eyes. He felt ashamed. Mothy wasn't wrong and his gentle tone made it harder to fight him about it.

"I know. Fine. I understand."

Mothy gave a half-cocked smile and kicked Wolflock in the foot.

"I don't think you do. I think I know how to get you to understand though. It's how Ma taught me to think about others before I spoke. I want you to tell me about me."

"What?"

"What would you do if you had to tell someone those things about me? Go on. Have a good look and tell me what you see."

"Why? I mean, I will do it, but why?"

"Because we're friends. People are kinder and more honest and more thoughtful when they're speaking to a friend. You kind of see everyone else as beneath you, don't you?"

Wolflock's eyes widened, and he pursed his lips again. "I... well... they are not as smart as me and they bore me so much."

"It's not their life's mission to amuse you, Lockie. Everyone has value. Every single person and being can do good in this world. Everyone has a story that they think is the most important one. If you help them celebrate their story and listen without judgement, a whole new energy... a whole new world opens up to you. Now, go on, use your trick on me."

Wolflock's pensive face gazed over his friend, the

words sinking into him. Surely those people didn't have as much to offer as Mothy was giving them credit for. For the first time though, he looked at his friend critically.

He had an accent that focused his speech in between the front of his mouth and nose, suggesting he was raised in South Quarenth or Chalongesh and his dusty blond hair was fine and thin. His round face was by no means chubby, but he had a wide-set bone structure, again, common in Southern Chalongesh. Wolflock had seen him move with the agility of a dancer and he seemed to sneak about a lot, as well as know many secrets. He also got along well with everyone, as if he'd been trained in sales, and had navigated the society of a large family or close-knit village. His oversized clothes were made of practical fabric. They were made of woven hemp, but he had worn them so much that the sleeves and hems were frayed. His shoes were of high-quality leather, but they had also seen many years of use. Sometimes he wore a brown vest that was a few shades different from his trousers and shoes, showing that he had obtained each piece at different times. He wore no jewellery and only had a plain belt. He had no personalised objects. He had an old brush by his bedside table he never used because when he woke, he'd just run his fingers through his hair, and it would fall into place. No books, no pens, nothing. Mothy truly was everything he was in that present moment.

"Uh... Hmm... I feel like this is cheating because I know you personally," Wolflock mumbled awkwardly, rubbing his arm.

Mothy just smiled. "That's fine. Tell me what you see. At least I won't chase you around the ship trying to get blood out of a stone."

"Well, you grew up in a large family around the South. Many siblings you were the eldest to. You'd often have to navigate them to keep harmony. Your mother was a great teacher, and I assume your father was a salesman. I didn't think there were many gypsy bands down in Quarenth, but I get the impression that you travelled a lot, having to sell things to locals and find out information about them, sometimes having to steal?" Wolflock offered gently, not wanting to call Mothy a thief.

"I called it borrowing." Mothy laughed through his nose and touched the back of his neck in embarrassment.

"Your family is very practical though. They bought you clothes that you should grow into and you have had them for a long time, so they are of great quality. Very durable. You did not grow up in affluence which is why your family probably had to save for your clothing, but you were around a few people that were wealthy, which is why you are able to converse with everyone. You must have had a very happy childhood, though. You are always smiling and happy. Everyone enjoys your company and you share that happiness with everyone you meet. Only the most blessed and pleasant of childhoods could create that in a person."

"You'd hope so," Mothy smiled, closing his eyes and tilting his head to the side.

"Did I get anything wrong?"

"Nope! All spot on! Well done." He put both of his hands behind his head, "But you see how you delivered it with more delicacy? You don't think you can try that with other people, do you?"

"I fail to see the point. They are not my friends and offer me no benefit to exerting the energy. It was quite tiresome to do it even for you."

Mothy abruptly burst out laughing so hard he cried.

"Oh, Lockie! Oh, you're a riot! You'll get it someday I hope-Ow!"

Mothy had reached forward to give Wolflock's foot a playful wobble, but his sleeve caught the candle flame and the tattered ends lit up rapidly.

Wolflock shoved the candle aside and helped Mothy tear his shirt off. He dumped the pitcher of water upside down, dousing the flames and sending a billow of steam and smoke out of the crate. They stumbled out of their hiding spot and coughed from the smoke. Catching each other's eye, their coughing turned into bouts of laughter.

"Oh, my goodness!" Mothy wheezed. "We could have set the whole ship on fire!"

"We could have died!" Wolflock could barely get a word out through his gasping laughs.

Mothy doubled over and Wolflock saw it.

He grabbed his friend by the shoulder and whirled him around in the dim light of the hull. What he saw horrified him. A gigantic ugly scar in the shape of an eye with a cross through its middle and a middle branch that extended all the way down his spine covered his friend's entire back, ending in a large X. It stretched from shoulder to shoulder and all the way down to the top of his trousers.

"Mothy..." Wolflock breathed.

"What? Is there a blister?"

"Mothy what is this?" Wolflock traced it, barely able to touch it at all.

"Huh? What's what? Oh!" Mothy snorted and ran his fingers through his hair. "It's just a birthmark, Lockie. Weird looking, isn't it?"

"Mothy... that is not a-"

"What in Houl's name is going on down here?!"

"Grogen I told yeh, I smell smoke!"

Before Wolflock could say another word Grogen and Goden thumped down the stairs and looked at the boys in alarm.

"Yeh got three seconds to tell me why I smell smoke on a wooden ship or I'm gettin' the Cap'in!" Grogen eyed them warningly.

"It was my fault, Grogen," Mothy stepped forward and hugged his arms. "I had a candle going and my shirt caught it. We were just messing around."

Grogen's hard look softened, and he took off his huge vest, wrapping it around Mothy's shoulders.

"Ah, yeh foolish lads. Fire is tha worst possible thing yeh can do on a ship. Why'd yeh think the kitchen's so protected? Get both of yeh to yeh rooms. No dinner feh either of yeh."

Mothy just smiled brightly like he always did, but Wolflock followed them up the stairs, his thoughts racing like a fly caught in a web. He was sure he'd gotten the details right... but as he bid Mothy a cautious 'good night' he realised how old that scar looked. Wolflock had seen burn scars before. Soldiers returned from the war eight years ago and their burns looked about the same as that. That meant Mothy had been scarred when he was around seven. Maybe younger. Wolflock absentmindedly put his slippers on, took them off again and got half undressed for bed.

You must have had a very happy childhood, though. You are always smiling and happy. Everyone enjoys your company and you share that happiness with everyone you meet. Only the most blessed and pleasant of childhoods could create that in a person.

That's what he'd said...

An image of the horses they raised flashed across his mind as he meditated on what he'd seen.

Their horses were happy, well trained and loved... but some of the others they took in had come from dreadful employers. Abusive, cruel and sadistic...

Then it struck him so hard he sat bolt upright in bed, his skin chilled with horror. Mothy's strange marking wasn't a scar.

It was a brand.

Everything he'd told Mothy... everything Mothy had

confirmed.

   It was a lie.

CHAPTER 3

Research

Wolflock barely slept. Every time he closed his eyes, he saw the scar. The brand. The burning hot branding iron in the shape of the eye and cross. He couldn't stop seeing his friend in agony. What had it been like? What had caused it? Was Mothy part of a cult? Was he a criminal? Was it an accident?

Wolflock racked his brain for answers but found none. Yet there was a terrible sense that he had seen that symbol somewhere before. He slept for a short time and woke again, desperately wanting to question Mothy further. He needed to know.

His mental web began to form with Mothy at the centre, but no strand connected to anything. Everything was a guess and not even a plausible guess at this stage. It was as if his mental web was fluttering about in the wind, waiting for something to stick.

The sun finally began to rise and Wolflock woke to the chilly blue light turning pink as the day sleepily rose around him. The ship was silent besides the splashing of waves against the sides, but Wolflock couldn't rest. He washed his face and dressed himself for the cool day ahead, still in a haze from the lack of sleep. Unable to focus his thoughts to their usual clarity, he decided that a walk around the deck would help ease his mind.

It served the exact opposite.

As he walked in the lonely silence, he couldn't help but go over the details of his friend with even more scrutiny. There were so many little things he hadn't taken into consideration during their time in the crate. Solid things that began to build the inner evidence of his mental web.

For starters, Mothy constantly smiled, but Wolflock had noted flashes of fear whenever anyone raised their voice or grew angry. If people were arguing in earnest, Mothy was either nowhere to be seen, as if he'd vanished into thin air, or he inserted himself right in the middle like a diplomatic wedge, soothing the confrontation.

He was also resourceful with all manner of odd items or places. He knew where most of the secret passageways and cupboards were on the ship and was able to improvise any object into a useful tool. Wolflock had seen him pick a chest lock when Veluse lost his key, with merely a nail and a stick. He'd seen him make a needle and thread out of fish bone and loose strands of rope, all to fix Tinni's sleeve before her mother saw it. Mothy had even used a broken piece of an old barrel to gut a fish two days before.

He kept everything he owned stashed in his bag at all times, only taking out one item or two and putting them back soon after being done with them. It was like he thought he'd need to leave at any moment.

Then there were the strange scars Wolflock had noticed. All along his arms and one thin silver line across his cheek. Most of them were so faded that they were hard to make out, but Wolflock had seen his friend from most angles and was perceptive enough to observe them.

Finally, there was the unusual fact that he wrote to no one, even though he could read and write perfectly well. Wolflock thought he would be constantly sending letters back home to his huge family, but Mothy never once moved to a pen.

After circling the deck for a few laps, Wolflock felt eyes on him. He glanced up to see the comforting smile of Captain Blutro at the helm, steering the ship through the peaceful waters.

"Good morning, Mr Felen. Pleased to see you're keeping up with regular exercise."

"Good morning, Captain. Were you steering all evening?" Wolflock stepped up the stairs next to the tall man dressed in his high collar jacket, his snuffle curled up at the back of his neck.

Wolflock patted the snuffle and gazed with a furrowed brow out across the deck.

"Aye. Slavidus will take over after breakfast. You caused quite a stir yesterday. Are you well? I'm dreadfully sorry they chased you about like thugs. Unfortunately, you offended them all quite severely." The Captain's bold voice seemed a touch rough with fatigue.

"Hmm? Oh. I suppose I did. Thank you for stopping them, I guess." He shrugged and looked away, his cheeks flushing.

"I don't believe you meant it. Youth causes a lack

of empathy for others. Everything in your world is only about you. You only truly see beyond your horizons when you're in your late second decade. Unless, of course, you've been through terrible circumstances. But you've been pampered most of your life, so I expect it will strike you later that others feel as you do."

Wolflock frowned in thought. "And what would that do? Having been through terrible circumstances?"

"Lad... I've seen people from all walks of life. Empathy is one of the most underappreciated gifts we have. A wretched life does one of two things in my experience. It either turns you into a self-pitying monster who gives neither hide nor hair for anyone else's needs or feelings. Or it makes you care for everyone, even the damned. You want to save everyone from the pain that you were caused as a way of healing your own hurts."

"Clearly both are undesirable, but how do you stop from becoming the monster?"

Captain Blutro smiled wisely and raised his face to the first glowing sunbeams splitting across the trees.

"You realise everyone has a story and that every story has value. Everyone thinks they are doing the right thing and that they are the hero. If you understand them and their story, you know what they're made of and how to help them become better."

"That's pretty profound talk for a man who is about to go to bed," Wolflock snorted.

"Aye. But that's when the best ideas break through. Or the worst. I did once mistake my niece for a goblin in this state."

"How did that work out?"

"It didn't. She hasn't spoken to me since. Fickle lass. What was I meant to think with her walking about with some strange mud concoction on her face?"

Wolflock chuckled, and they fell into a comfortable silence. Then the image of the scar on Mothy's back blazed into his mind again and he grimaced.

"Uh... Captain?" he coughed.

"Yes, Mr Felen?"

"I saw a symbol, and I was wondering if you knew what it may be."

"Oh?"

"Yes... Um... oh! Here-" Wolflock pulled the charcoal pencil he'd forgotten to take from his pocket the day before and began drawing the eye and cross with the X at the base on his hand.

When he looked up the Captain's face was dark.

All traces of sleepy playfulness had vanished, and he looked disgusted at the symbol.

"Aye. I've seen it before. Where did you see it? I won't have any of that on my ship."

"I didn't see it on the ship," Wolflock backtracked immediately. Was Mothy something horrific? Was this a criminal sign? Was he a pirate?

Captain Blutro's shoulders relaxed, and he sighed. "Those sorts of things aren't for young gentlemen to know about. I just pray you never have to meet anyone who worships that symbol. I don't like speaking poorly of any faith. Gods know we have so many across the land. But that one... It's not natural."

"It's a religious symbol?"

Captain Blutro nodded, sighing again. "Aye. Of sorts. It's an old faith. As you should know, most of our faiths across the land are to respect our residential gods. On the river we worship Houl, the god who is the river and protects it. We barter safe passage by keeping it clear and never taking more than he rightly provides. When we get to the Silver Lake, the gods there change. When you're in Mystentine, they'll likely worship the Shiriling goddess of knowledge. This symbol... it belongs to a group who think there aren't local gods. That their god is the one and only. That all other gods are false and that anyone who worships them is lesser. They... they have cruel practices to magic users and women. And anyone who isn't pale skinned. They're just cruel and every time I meet one, they seem sick with an unhealthy love of their 'lord'."

"They sound like the Trostons. There's a small sect of them in Plugh. The Queen said anyone can practice their faith as long as it does no harm. They seem harmless enough," Wolflock interjected, thinking of how the Trostons had a similar symbol, but it was only a 't' with an arch over the top three lines.

"Aye. Trostons are normally harmless. We had a priest of Trost on for a week at the start of the journey. He just wore all black and spoke like a normal gent. There were unrecorded sections of the old Trostons from hundreds of years ago though. They broke away from the regulated and peaceful core. They were spurred on by insane men I heard. The symbol was corrupted and now anyone who bares any variation of the mark of Trost with pride is nothing but a monster. Don't underestimate them, Wolflock. The Trost variations can be cunning, ruthless and always have an evil agenda."

"Duly noted, Captain. I've never heard of these

cults though."

"They stay very quiet, lad."

"How do you know about them then?"

"We had one on here a few years back. We found his companion beaten to death in their room. He forced the poor man to sleep on the floor, wouldn't let him come to certain meals or talk to anyone else. He wore a necklace with that symbol on it. Then I started hearing rumours from the other passengers about him after he was detained. They were all too scared to say anything until he was off the ship because they thought he would do the same to them. I was ashamed we didn't attend to it all before the tragedy."

"How were you to know? If no one speaks up, then you cannot expect to see it. Only people who had seen it before would recognise it..." Wolflock mumbled. "Captain?"

"Aye?"

"What do you know about Mothy? Where did he grow up?"

"Judging by his accent, South Chalongesh. Why? You two are thick as thieves. I thought you'd know everything about him by now."

"I did ask him, but I don't think he wants to talk

about it." It's not like he outright lied to me, Wolflock thought with sour sarcasm.

Blutro turned the spoked wheel as they meandered up the river, the forests on either side of the bank growing thicker and wilder.

"Can't say I've had too much time to talk about his past. But if anyone would know about him, it would be Froderyk and Fuhji, Dlumi and the Blickland sisters. He boarded with Ungul and Uhnha at Shellinden, so they probably know him best."

"And the others?" Wolflock sighed, full of despondency.

"Let's see... he was the only one who could break Dlumi out of her silent, sad mood a few ports before Corl and he helped Fuhji and Froderyk sneak away from some unsavoury folk when they first boarded. Sent them on a wild goose chase, apparently. I didn't hear the conversation though. If you made amends with them, you may get your answers."

Wolflock scowled at the Captain. "And they are your careful selection of people who know Mothy best on the ship, yes?"

"Aye."

"Of course they are. I see your game Captain."

"And what game would that be, Mr Felen?" Captain Blutro's mouth twitched with a smirk.

"The game of you trying to get me to apologise to the others. Mothy plays the same game."

The Captain laughed from his belly. "Well, I guess we both only play games we can win. I can smell breakfast. Go and fill your belly, Mr Felen. See how well you can play my game."

Wolflock stalked off, feeling bitter that the Captain's supposed wisdom was all a ploy to make him forego his pride for the sake of those idiots.

Well, I will not suffer even an inch of it! He thought furiously and banged into the dining hall.

He had ignored how his stomach had gnawed on itself, punishing him for missing dinner the night before. Only a few people had made their way to breakfast this early and as he glanced around, he saw the Nan family silently eating their porridge, adding spices that made it smell mouth-watering. The only other occupants were Hognut, one of the crewmen, and Slavidus.

Wolflock collected a bowl of porridge and walnuts, sat down and glared at everyone. More people slowly made their way to their morning meal, and he glared at them too.

How dare they all ignore me? I will show them. I will show them all. They have not seen how clever I am. They will not be able to call me stupid ever again. It is just like Plugh all over again...

No one made eye contact with him and most people pretended he didn't exist. It was horrible. It would have been better if everyone told him off or interacted with him in any way. His anger subsided into a low seethe and by the time Mothy dragged himself sleepily to the table, he felt a peculiar sad feeling that Wolflock was familiar with but didn't have a name for.

Shame? No. It could not be. I'm not ashamed of anything. I acted perfectly fine.

"G'mornin' Lockie. Sleep well?" Mothy yawned.

"Yes. Fine. You?"

"Like a dead fish.

"I wanted to talk to you about something." He had to know if Captain Blutro was right. Was it a sign of evil doers? His friend had been so kind, so jovial, so agreeable. Surely, he wasn't part of some strange cult to a ruthless god.

Mothy hummed as he filled his face with one of his porridge bowls.

"Yesterday. In the crate. What was that symbol?"

Mothy swallowed his food and took another mouthful as if he wasn't going to answer at first, but Wolflock stared at him with such a sincere concern that the blond boy finished and smiled back, scratching his nose.

"I'm sure I don't know what you mean. It's just a birthmark, maybe?"

"You... you know I know you lied to me. Did I get anything about your history correct?" Wolflock blinked, leaning back in disbelief that Mothy was still lying.

"What do you mean, Lockie? It's nothing."

"That is a brand. Like what bad ranchers do to livestock. But that is burnt into you... It is so old. How old were you when that happened?" Wolflock pushed, desperate to know more and horrified that Mothy had continued to lie so easily to him.

He sighed and leaned forward on his elbows, staring into the space between his clasped hands. A heavy energy blanketed them and Wolflock could barely hear the chatter of people around them. "It's in my past. Just a nasty souvenir. Long story really."

Wolflock leaned forward and pressed his shoulder comfortingly to Mothy's, waiting. "I think we have time and I'd like to hear it."

Mothy rolled his eyes and chuckled as he scratched his temple with a calloused finger, breaking the feeling that had fallen over them as if he'd ripped off a wound dressing. "I fell into a hot iron when I lived in Southern Chalongesh. Stupid really. Very embarrassing, but I was only four when it happened."

"I feel like that's a lie too. I could see it when your eyes moved to the left and your smile flickered into anger."

"Oh, do you now?" Mothy smirked and raised an eyebrow.

"Yes. I studied facial movements when I watched father's business dealings and visiting politicians. Glancing to your left is a creative thought; to the right is a factual one. Given you're right handed. If you were left handed it may be swapped."

Mothy nodded in appreciation of Wolflock's intellect, but his lips stayed shut.

Until he took another mouthful of food.

"Where did you get that mark? In Chalongesh?"

Mothy chewed.

Wolflock waited.

"Are you religious, Lockie?" he finally spoke through his mouthful.

"Not particularly. I will abide by any local rules and activities for their gods out of respect, but I follow no tenants."

Mothy nodded and continued eating.

"Religion forms a community that many people thrive off and sometimes encourages them to do beautiful things. Artwork, charity, that kind of thing. When I was in Shellinden, the temple of the Moon Dragon healed so many sick people. All because it was part of their practices."

"I fail to see why they cannot do it without religion. It is perfectly acceptable for people to just act in kindness and consideration of their fellows."

"A bit like speaking kindly and considerately to one's fellow shipmates." Mothy jabbed his elbow into Wolflock's arm. "Some people need permission to do things. Especially if it's a bit bold or forthright."

"You don't though do you?" Wolflock smirked, thinking of their first meeting and how Mothy had helped him break the rules of the ship.

"It's just not in my nature. If rules don't make sense or stop me from having harmless fun, then why bother remembering them?"

"That is clearly why we are friends. What is your

nature, though?"

"To do the right thing. Even if it isn't the legal thing. Sometimes those who set the rules don't care for the pain they cause. They can be... what was it... devoid of reality."

"Did your mother teach you that?"

Mothy scrunched up his face and picked at his teeth. "Listen, Lockie. If you want to start pulling out 'mother' jokes, then you're going to lose. I learned so many jokes about mothers you'll be peeing yourself laughing before you can finish a punchline. For example: Your mother is so ugly she couldn't marry a troll."

Wolflock blinked.

"I... you have never seen... oh! I get it!"

He chuckled a little and Mothy's smile brightened, but somehow his eyes stayed quite flat.

"See? Peeing yourself. I told Hognut I'd help him in the kitchen today if he'd give me a few sweets later. Want to join us?"

"Uh... I think I'm fine. I don't have a sweet tooth like you."

"Of course you don't. I'll speak to you later."

Mothy rolled his eyes and collected their bowls, heading over to Hognut, who seemed quite surprised by the offer of assistance.

Wolflock understood though.

Mothy didn't want to talk about any of this with him, but the pain that he had glimpsed in his friend's façade made Wolflock even more determined to find the truth. Had he run away from the cult? Was someone hunting him? Why had he asked if Wolflock was religious?

Even more web strands whipped about him with no answers to latch onto.

He knew one thing though. He'd have to get answers from the five people he wanted nothing to do with if he had any hope of finding the truth.

As he watched after his friend, the door to the outside deck opened and Uhnha came in with Ungul at her arm.

"Ungul!" Wolflock called out. The room fell tensely silent. "I have questions and you have the answers. Tell me what I need to know, now!"

Ungul's face contorted into a blended grin and snarl.

"You want answers, little boy?" She spoke like deep velvet with a thick accent. "The only thing you'll get answers from is my foot on your throat."

Rhiannon D. Elton

CHAPTER 4

Pass or Fail

She wouldn't hit him. He knew it. She wasn't allowed. Wolflock barged up to her and stomped his foot. "You know about Mothy and I want you to tell it to me. Do it now or-"

"Or what, little boy?" she hissed.

Uhnha's wide nose was wrinkled in distaste at his presence, but she put her hand on her sister's arm and looked down at him. "He's not worth the energy sister. He is just a rude little boy."

"Tell me about Mothy when you first met him," Wolflock demanded.

Ungul snorted.

"I said tell me!"

Her face changed when he didn't budge. Instead of finding him irritably entertaining as she had a moment before, he was now a bug in her way.

"Uhnha, go eat. This one needs a lesson."

"A lesson? What on earth do you–Ah! Put me down!"

Ungul stood to her full height of six and a half feet and picked Wolflock up by the scruff. He flung his arms and legs about wildly, but she had him incapacitated. Her iron vice grip on the back of his vest saved him from choking on his shirt collar but the discomfort under his arms was quite inconsiderate as far as he was concerned.

"Let go of me you brute! Release me at once!" he shouted.

Ungul walked him outside in silence and up to the helm where Slavidus and the Captain were changing shifts.

"What's all this?" Slavidus stared in alarm.

Ungul threw Wolflock forward, causing him to tumble hard on the deck.

"This wretched imp has been harassing my sister and I. I would like to make a formal complaint."

The Captain sighed and shook his head, his face weary. "Of course, Ungul. I shan't have passengers troubling each other aboard my vessel. What can he do the rectify the situation?"

Ungul snarled, her pristine white teeth bared. "He can stay as far away from my sister and I as possible."

"Unfortunately, the vessel isn't shaped for that. Any other suggestions?"

"Put him in the hull. No one on the ship likes this vermin, anyway."

Wolflock winced as if she'd hit him.

That is not true. Tanni, Tinni, Mothy, Captain Blutro... they all like me.

"Now, now, Ungul. Mr Felen is a passenger of the Silver Ice Hair and no matter how uncouth his manners can be, he is still owed all the courtesies, as are any of my passengers and crew. The hull is out of the question. What can be done to resolve your feelings for him? Or at least to lessen them? We are in an isolated space on the ship and creating harmony is our highest priority."

Ungul rolled her eyes. "You could let me hang him over the side of the ship and scare the mischief from his mouth."

Wolflock's jaw dropped. "What?!"

Captain Blutro wobbled his head from side to side as if he were considering it.

"You cannot be serious!"

Captain Blutro shook his head after some deliberation and chuckled. "You know what, Ungul? Take the day to think about what actions Mr Felen can do to improve your feelings and come back to me at dinner when I wake up. Have your answer by then and we'll figure things out. If you have not thought of anything by the time dinner comes, I'll think of the matter as resolved."

Slavidus took the helm and the Captain bid them good day.

Wolflock sighed with relief. This was the easiest way to avoid punishment, and he silently commended the Captain for his diplomacy. He was sure that Ungul was too thick to think of anything besides doing one or two activities for him. That would fix it all up and he could resume his search for Mothy's history. His smile dropped when he turned to Ungul.

She was grinning wickedly from ear to ear. Her bright white teeth gleaming against her obsidian skin. Her black eyes glinting with malice.

"Uh..."

"I know what I'll have you do. You can be the manservant for everyone on the ship to show them your charity and make up for the hurt you've caused."

"Oh? Is that all? A few days of that won't be too hard-"

"A few days?" She cackled. "Until the journey ends at Creast is what I'll say! You'll learn humility that way!"

She walked passed him holding her belly as she laughed. The stone of realisation hit the pit of his stomach. Wolflock had a horrible image pass through his mind of him having to clean Hognut's toenails while being yelled at by three people for not folding their clothes correctly, not tucking their sheets in and tending their bedpans in the middle of the night. By the time they reached Creast, he would have aged from the hard labour. Surely, he'd look like he was ninety! The worst image that peeped through his mind though, and the one that surprised him most, was seeing Mothy still pretending to be happy. It was if he could see an inner Mothy through the pretense and the one within was in pain. He had to find out the source of that pain... even if he didn't yet know why.

If he was working from dawn to dusk every day, he'd have so little time to find out what he needed to about his friend.

"W-wait! Ungul, Ungul. Ungul!" he pleaded, darting after her and pulling her enormous hand to stop her step.

She turned and looked down at him fearsomely.

"Please! Please, I'm not staff. I will just upset people more if you tell the captain that! And you know he'll accept your offer because for some crazy reason he loves hard work. Please reconsider! I'll die from that much labour! Please! I'll do anything!"

"Begging to avoid punishment? Pathetic."

"No, no! I promise I'll do the thing you say, but please shorten the sentence. Can we please make it three days? Even a week!"

Ungul's nose wrinkled in disgust.

"Why would I give any allowances for you, a little rude boy?"

Wolflock's mind zoomed in on every detail of her being. Her bright clothes, her tight braids, her stern features. He had to find something that would make her crack just enough to save him from his sentencing. Beads in her braids, particular weaves in the details of her clothes, a locket that didn't match her attire? With a translucent smoothed salt gem.

Salt.

Shellinden.

She boarded with Mothy.

The Captain said she would know Mothy best.

"I'm doing this for Mothy."

Ungul's face didn't so much soften as it became less creased.

"Why?"

"We're going to Mystentine together and I want to get to know him better. I want to make sure he's... happy. Surely you can see it too? You've known him for longer than anyone on the ship. His sadness and hurt leeches through his constant smiles. I just wanted to help make his smiles real."

It wasn't a total lie. He did want to find out what was going on under Mothy's façade, he just didn't know why and having a pretense was sure to help reduce the punishment Ungul would ask for. Even though Ungul stood up straighter and folded her arms, Wolflock could see her defenses had cracked. Then he did something he shouldn't have. Something he couldn't control.

He smiled.

Ungul's face darkened and furrowed with suspicion.

"If you are truly serious and not doing this only to escape servitude to the ship, you will do this thing I ask. If you complete the task, I will reduce your punishment to only a week. Because I do not believe you, because I see your true eyes, I do not think you can manage it."

"What is it? What would you have me do?"

"Before I speak to the Captain this evening, you must find Mothy's middle name."

"His middle name?"

"Yes. If you're as clever as you think you are, it should be easy. Do this before I speak to the Captain at dinner and I'll ask for your punishment to be reduced to a week instead of the rest of the journey."

"This will be simple. I'll be back within the hour," Wolflock nodded, determination flaring in his eyes and he whipped around to rush back to the dining hall.

Mothy was still chatting with Hognut, kicking his heels on the cabinet door and eating a long strip of sugared ginger. He turned to Wolflock and smiled, the long strip of golden ginger dangling out of his mouth like a strange tongue.

"Lockie! Oh!" He smiled and waved, but when he spoke the ginger fell out and he snatched at it with both hands like someone losing something slippery from their grasp.

Putting it back in his wide mouth he just grinned, clenching his teeth so as not to lose it again.

"Mothy! I have a dire question for you. It's a matter of my back breaking or not."

"Someone's going to break your back? Sounds serious. Is it Ungul? At least she'd do it quickly. I've heard breaking backs doesn't hurt at all... That may have been for the back breaker though. Not the back breakee."

"I need to know your full name."

Mothy blinked. "Uh... why exactly?"

Wolflock deliberated for a second in his mind. Surely, he could trust Mothy to tell him what he needed to know. Mothy loved helping people and if Wolflock was worked to the bone on the ship for the next two months he'd lose his best source of company. Mothy would want to help him but he should be honest.

"Ungul is going to ask the Captain to make me work as a crewman for the duration of the journey if I can't tell her your full name. It's a test, apparently. Silly woman didn't think we were close enough friends, but I know you'll have my back, aye?" Wolflock nodded eagerly.

Mothy's eyes went a little wide and his cheeks flushed pink. He glanced at Hognut, who was scrubbing the only remaining pot while humming a river chanty, then back at Wolflock.

"So, what is it? I cannot believe I don't know your full name and we've known each other a week."

"Mmmm... I was sure I told you." He took his ginger strip out of his mouth and scratched the back of his head. "My name is Mothy Enitnelav."

"Enitnelav? That sounds like a variation of the name Nelav in Quarenth."

"Innit though?" Mothy half laughed with his thickest South Chalongesh accent.

"What about your middle name?" Wolflock pressed, leaning on the bench next to him to try to appear relaxed.

"I thought only wealthy people had middle names? Nope. I'm just Mothy Enitnelav." He was persistently scratching his head as if he had lice.

"So, you don't have a middle name? That's why Ungul thought this would be a clever trick. Very well. It has been an absolute pleasure meeting you Mr Enitnelav. Thank you kindly for releasing me from my punishment."

"Yah welcome prince." Mothy gave a jaunty fist pump and hopped off the bench. "I'm off for a stroll. Want to come?"

"Nay, my friend. I must finish this task and then write to my sister. I'll find you when I'm done and we'll celebrate. I wouldn't mind seeing if we could fly with some of the old sails in the hull."

"Dangerous." Mothy nodded in approval. "See you later, then."

Wolflock nodded and hurried out to catch Ungul, but she wasn't on the forward deck.

She must have gone back to her room.

He grinned happily to himself, quite proud of how he'd solved yet another case in record time. Of course, he'd have to boast to Myna about how real-world experience indubitably surpasses their sheltered home life mysteries. He glanced into Ungul and Uhnha's room, seeing only Uhnha napping with her back to him.

Did I miss her on the deck? She must be at the back behind the dining hall.

Wolflock rolled his eyes and stomped back upstairs, certain he knew where she was now. As he approached the back of the dining hall, he heard Ungul talking.

"... you cannot deny a whole part of yourself. It is cowardly, and you are not a coward."

"Ungul, you had no right to tell him anything about that. I left it behind, and I never wanted to speak about it again, let alone have him question me about it. You know how clever he is!"

Wolflock pressed himself to the edge of the dining hall, his spine tingling with realisation as Mothy spoke.

"I know how rude he is. Either way, he will lose this and be forced to work. It should teach him some humility."

"But why did you shove me in the middle? I've done nothing wrong and I've been your friend this whole time. I helped you find Uhnha when-"

"It was the only thing I could think of that he would never succeed at."

"It was unkind. You were only thinking of your own anger at him and you were unkind to me..."

"Oh, my darling, no! No, no, no! That was not my intention at all. There now, don't be upset. He'll believe you above me. He'll do his month's work and that will be the end of it."

Wolflock heard Mothy sigh loudly, more strained than he'd ever seen before.

"I hope so. I forgive you, but I would rather no more be spoken about this. Just tell him he's right with whatever he answers and let it be that."

"What? No. I'll be telling him he's wrong and he'll serve his full month as he deserves! He slighted my sister!"

"Then you'll condemn my past to come to light."

"If you love him as much as you say you do, then you'll be honest with him. But I know you don't. So, he will work."

Mothy growled in frustration. "That has nothing to do with any of this. He's my friend, just as you are. I guess this teaches me to never reveal anything to anyone ever again. Fine... Do what you will, but know that I only allow this to persist because it aids your sister."

Wolflock pressed himself down amongst the crates and watched Mothy's lanky form stalk passed, his fists clenched and his face red. He'd lied again.

Wolflock felt a stab to his chest with the very thought. He believed Mothy and him to be good friends and yet here it was. Mothy. Lying to him. But for what reason? Did he belong to a cult at some stage and his name reflected it? Was he still part of it? Was there a greater scheme at hand that Mothy was set to orchestrate and maintain anonymity?

Wolflock stared into space, elbows on knees, as the pieces of the web in his mind flew about like streamers in a gale. Mothy was at the centre and his mysterious life blew around him, but instead of accidentally whipping out of reach of Wolflock's hands, he now saw it as being intentionally guarded from him.

He couldn't ask Mothy for the answers anymore.

What if something larger was at play here? He had to find out.

He'd have to speak to those he'd offended. He'd have to use his deductive skills in a way he'd never done so before.

He'd have to apologise.

CHAPTER 5

The Runaways

Wolflock's mind raced as he sat behind the rough wooden crate. He was as still as stone, barely blinking in the windless pocket of the ship. He had a precise ten hours until dinner and perhaps a few minutes extra while the Captain ate and Ungul talked. Even if he didn't find out all Mothy's secrets today and only accomplished finding his middle name, working like a dog on the ship would certainly stop him from finding out anything else. He had to get the answers. But how?

Froderyk, Dlumi, Ungul and Uhnha hated him.

This was undeniable. And yet...

Fuhji didn't hate him. She was also kind and may perhaps want to talk to him due to her husband stopping her from talking to anyone. Solitude had great powers of persuasion. He had to think of a way to get her talking. He remembered the Captain had mentioned that Mothy helped them both get onto the ship when they were being hunted in Corl. She also knew his cousin, Quathie...

That was it!

He scrambled to his feet and charged back into the dining hall. He threw the doors open with a dramatic bang and froze. Everyone in the hall stared at his unexpected gusto.

Unapologetically he began scanning the room.

Hognut, Tinni, Tanni, Stra, Nan Ji. Ahah!

Froderyk and Fuhji were rubbing their full bellies and having their customary fifth cup of tea as Wolflock approached.

"What do you want, boy?" Froderyk snarled and stood up from his chair.

Wolflock's first reaction was to sneer at the term boy, but he drew in a sharp breath and gritted his teeth. This was going to be harder than he thought.

"I wanted to come and speak to you about... earlier." He tried to smile, but it looked more like a strange grimace.

"Hmph! There is nothing to talk about. Now, be off with you."

"I wanted," Wolflock continued, feeling like a vein may burst in his head, "to apologise."

Fuhji smiled delightedly and Froderyk looked like someone had slapped him. He shook his head and blinked back into his anger.

"Did the Captain tell you to do this? I won't accept anything but a genuine apology."

"The Captain did not tell me to do this. I behaved poorly, and I would like to understand you both better, so I do not offend anyone else in the future."

Wolflock knew this was quite close to being an outright lie, but he had to. He had to know about Mothy. He had to reduce his punishment.

A few tense moments of Froderyk glaring at him, the burly man gestured to a chair and Wolflock took a seat next to Fuhji. He preferred to sit across from Froderyk, so he was not only out of arm's reach but also able to observe his tiniest movements.

"I..." he glanced at Fuhji from the corner of his eye and saw her face creased ever so slightly with maternal concern. "I don't really know how to do this, so please help me if I say the wrong thing. My father didn't have much of a chance to raise my sister and I with social delicacies since he worked so hard. I mean... it's not like my cousin Quathie. Both of her parents are there, and she's had you as a friend to help guide her through the intricate social dynamics of society."

If Wolflock had been an archer, he would have hit his target so precisely it would have pierced a blueberry.

Fuhji touched her heart and patted him on the back, clearly seeking to care and nurture his request for assistance. Wolflock had expected this. What he hadn't expected was the shoulders of Froderyk relaxing at the mention of a hard-working father.

"Well, that explains a lot." Froderyk nodded understandingly.

"Yes. I believe I wanted to say that I'm sorry, and I'd like to hear the tale of how you both came to this ship. It will not only help my deductive skills, but I hope I can be liked half as much as Mothy is by you both. I believe you're rather fond of him, yes?"

Fuhji gave Wolflock's shoulder a little squeeze. "Do you mind if I tell him our tale, my love? I do love our story so very much."

Froderyk leaned back and drew in a breath, nursing

his tea in thought. "We won't be stopping until we are beyond the mountains. And you did remind me I have been a bit unsavoury of late, even though we should be safe from the clutches of your family. If it will make you happy, my dear, go ahead. This may teach me how to tame our own children when I spend time at work too often."

"That was one of the things I fell in love with," Fuhji began with a sugared smile. "As you saw, I'm actually the only daughter of the Korsaki family. We travelled from Xiayah five generations ago and my family has always been strict with tradition. We came over as merchants and eventually managed all the grain within Quarenth. My brothers take care of it now, but I was intended for the Elivius family. They-"

"You were engaged to Jamus? Jamus Elivius? Son of the Gem Baron?"

Fuhji tittered and Froderyk scoffed.

"That would be him, yes. You know him?"

"I mean... we met occasionally. Father raised horses for him and trained their stable hands. We had dinner a few times with their family." Avoiding Froderyk's eye he added, "They're quite pompous and entitled though. Just because they were born to wealth doesn't mean they're better than anyone else."

"That's what I said!" Froderyk interjected, slapping the table with his large hand.

"We were engaged, but I found him boring. There was no passion. No vigour for life. I grew up in such strict circumstances and was always groomed to be the perfect daughter. Then one day, I was walking with my handmaiden through the market and we saw this big beautiful gentleman with his vest buttoned wrong-"

"I keep telling you it was in fashion to have it buttoned to the side more," Froderyk chuckled.

"-helping his staff set up their stalls and teaching a few runners to bring people over to the stallholders. One of them tripped and tipped over the whole table of wooden trinkets. The poor lad was terrified, but Froderyk didn't raise his voice like I'd seen Jamus do to staff. He scooped up the boy and soothed him, telling him that accidents happen and that was why they always kept glue in their packs."

"Revolutionary idea really. Keeping some fresh glue in case someone brought back broken bits and pieces. Just one of the services we offered to keep our people happy," Froderyk bustled as a half-cocked smile crept over his lips.

"I helped them clean up the mess, and Froderyk tended to me like a true gentleman. I was taken with him and he showed me excitement again. For months, we would meet in secret, just for the thrill of it. I believed that, due to his status as Jamus' main competitor, my family would be fine with swapping the engagement to him, but I was wrong. They moved the wedding forward as retaliation, telling me I was an undutiful daughter and that if I didn't marry Jamus, I would disgrace them all. On the eve of the wedding, Froderyk came to me and helped me escape. We cut my hair short and dressed me as a young man, and he made his excuses for leaving his businesses on such short notice. I was just upset I couldn't find my heirloom necklace. We bought passage on the Silver Ice Hair the very next morning, but it was set to sail hours later. Waiting was equally thrilling and anxiety-inducing."

"You can definitely say that again, my love."

"Most of the crew and company had gone ashore to buy goods and trinkets from the dock, except for Mothy who was too busy eating breakfast."

"I was grateful to see a familiar face," Froderyk nodded, sipping his tea.

"You'd met Mothy before the ship came to Corl?"

"Oh yes. Years ago. His guardian Hazzim and I met in Shellinden years ago. Hazzim and I talked for hours into the night about all kinds of business activities at a little party he had organised while the little lad played with my old dog, Bristles."

"That is fascinating! What was Mothy like as a child?"

Froderyk pinched his chin and looked up, remembering the night. "He was a tiny thing. Weedy. Wearing baggy clothes. A bit quiet and watched everything. Not shy though. He asked me all kinds of questions and answered everything with a star-struck look in his eyes. Bristles loved him though. He was a very gentle lad. He still is, rather."

"You said 'guardian'. Was he being taught by Hazzim? Where did they meet?"

"I only saw them for an evening. Hazzim just said Mothy was his 'ward' and we left it at that. I was more interested in getting better business advice. Then again, when we boarded the ship."

"I met Mothy when we boarded the ship. Froderyk was so surprised to see him."

"He'd grown a lot in those few years. Sprung up like a sapling!" Froderyk gestured with his index finger from table height to where Mothy's height was presently.

"We hid on the ship but Jamus' and my family's guard demanded they were allowed to search aboard for us. Mothy was so clever. He hid us in a box in the hull when the Captain questioned the guards. He sat on the box as they searched and asked them all kinds of irritating questions. Do you remember what he said, darling? Oh, his silly accent made me nearly laugh out loud."

"I recall but you do a better impression of him than me."

"They were searching closer and closer and Mothy started saying," Fuhji put her hands on her chair and impersonated a most innocent looking scoundrel with a thick cockney accent, "'so who yah looking for?' and the guard responded, 'none of your business, lad.' And Mothy replied, 'Oh, I know them! Nun-o-ya-bizness-lad is a good friend of mine. Bloody trouble maker they is though. Can't leave two bob laying about wit' them round. D'ya know their father?' The guard was so stumped with Mothy's response. All he could do was ask, 'What are you prattling on about?'. And Mothy said–and this is what really got me–Mothy said, 'Yeah. Their father. My-ship-my-bizness-lad?'. Oh, he's a daring young man! The guard rounded on him. We heard him stomp over and say, 'What did you just say to me?', and Mothy, as cool as a fresh apple, just said as innocently as ever, 'you want that pair that come on board right? The man and pretty woman? How much is that worth to ya?' I thought for sure he was going to give us up!"

"I was just about ready to throttle them all."

"'Ten coins.' The guard said-"

"We are worth so much more than ten coins," Froderyk sniffed indignantly.

"-and Mothy ummed and ahhed for a bit, then finally said, 'and that pretty necklace. I gots a sweetheart who'll love it.' The guard responded that he needed the necklace because it told him the general area we were in. Mothy laughed and said 'well yah won' need it when I tells yah where they is, so yah won' mind parting with it then will yah?' Somehow that chap is ever so convincing. The deal was struck and Mothy then said, 'well, when people norm'ly escape from 'ere they go South along the river 'cause no ships want that trouble that you're causin'. Not legal is it? Anyone on the run follows water South cause no one wants to go to the cold, do they? That's just logic innit? Now you gonna pay me? Now get ta racing! They left not two minutes afore you got on board! Yah better hurry on and catch 'em'."

"He's had our trust ever since."

"The moment they were gone he gave us the coins and the necklace. They'd been using magic to scry for us with my favourite heirloom necklace. Mothy knew what they were doing, and not only misdirected them but also stopped them from being able to find us before the ship set sail."

"He is always very kind. You've... actually helped me make sense of my original deductions. Thank you." Wolflock nodded slowly, piecing together the information and feeling an odd sensation in his chest. "And I am genuinely sorry for upsetting you earlier. I-"

"No excuses needed." Froderyk raised his hand to silence him. "I remember being a young man and not realising other people had feelings. Although I had it beaten out of me. I hope you learn before it's beaten out of you too."

"I am nothing if not a fast learner," Wolflock smirked.

"You're from Plugh, yes? Quathie spoke about the beautiful Mabon festivals they have there."

"Well, being in Grothener, the harvests give us an enormous bounty. Mabon was one of the better festivals."

"What kind of things do they give thanks for in

Plugh?" She asked.

"Uhh... I... I cannot really say for the rest of the town. Maybe food, lovers, wealth. Normal things."

"What were you thankful for?"

Wolflock felt his cheeks flush a little. "I... I was thankful for my horse and my library."

"That's very sweet."

Awkward as he felt, Wolflock smiled.

"I should probably go. I need to continue to make amends. Thank you for talking with me." He rose to shake both their hands.

"It was quite nice to talk about our journey until this point."

"Oh, yes!" Fuhji sighed with enthusiasm. "It was lovely. Come sit with us at dinner tonight with Mothy and we'll talk about changes that have occurred in Corl since you were last there."

Fuhji and Froderyk's faces were both soft, smiling and glowing with a fondness Wolflock wasn't accustomed to.

The proposition sounded rather boring, but the warm feeling in his gut dictated his words.

"That sounds lovely. I look forward to it."

He wasn't entirely sure what happened... but

something felt nice.

Rhiannon D. Elton

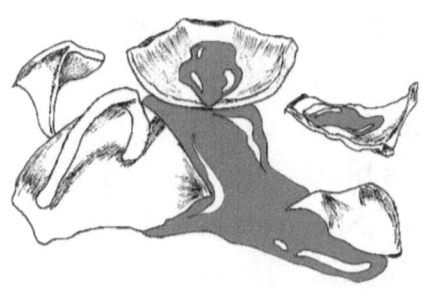

CHAPTER 6

The Dreamer

The creak of the pale grey planks of the ship and the sound of the wind battering against the white sails greeted Wolflock as he left the dining hall. The sun wasn't too far from the middle of the dazzling blue sky and he found himself wishing he could just sit and soak up the warmth for a bit longer. But he had to find Dlumi.

She hadn't been at breakfast and he hadn't seen her about the ship all day. Perhaps she wasn't well. Tea seemed to make everyone on board feel better, so Wolflock used the skills Mothy had shown him and brewed a simple cup before taking it to Dlumi's cabin.

The door was shut.

Wolflock knocked and tried to open it, but it was locked fast.

"Ms Dlumi? It's me, Mr Felen," he called through the door. "I was hoping to speak to you."

"Go away!" She grumbled loudly.

"I brought tea," he offered the tea to the door handle.

"I said go away!"

Wolflock frowned and pinched the bridge of his nose.

"Lockie?"

Wolflock nearly split the tea as he jumped, turning to see Mothy leaning against the banister with a raised eyebrow.

"What are you doing?"

"Mothy! It's just you. Phew. You startled me."

"What are you doing?" he repeated, nodding to Dlumi's door and the tea. Wolflock couldn't help but notice an air of suspicion about his person.

"I wanted to apologise to Dlumi for what I said and see if I could make amends."

Mothy's smile reached his eyes. "She'll warm up, eventually. She hasn't eaten all day."

"I resolved the confrontation with Froderyk and Fuhji. I'm on a bit of a roll and I'd like to keep it going. You know? To restore harmony as the Captain would say."

If Mothy's smile could grow any brighter, it did.

"Well, why didn't you say so? You're really doing this to make the whole ship happy? Well done! I'm proud of you! Not likely you'll get in there though. Not without going in through her window."

Wolflock said nothing, but he shrugged and puffed his chest out before the idea struck him.

"Mothy! You're a genius!"

He set the tea down by the door and dashed upstairs. Hopping from one foot to the other excitedly he glanced around the ship, finding a coil of rope and beginning to measure the distance between the stairwell and where Dlumi's room would be.

"So... What are you doing now?" Mothy asked with his arms folded. He'd followed him up and was watching Wolflock dash about with amusement.

"If I tie a rope to the railing here and climb down into Dlumi's room she'll have to speak to me. I know I can make this better if she'll just listen to me."

Mothy smirked. "I'm sure she will, but wouldn't it

have been more romantic if you'd sat outside her door, pining for her, moaning poetry and telling her how you love the powerful muscles of her-"

"No. I'll leave that to you, Mr Romance."

Mothy drew back in alarm and jerked his head. "Here. You're tying it wrong." He walked forward and untied Wolflock's work. "You're not trying to make the railing comfortable. You want to make sure it doesn't escape. If it does, you might get hurt."

He bound the rope around the railing so tightly that the paint flecked off, using his foot to draw it taut.

"What in Houl's name are yeh boys doin'?" Grunted a sour voice from behind them. Hognut was cleaning his ornate pipe and tipped the old contents over the railing.

"Swinging down in Dlumi's room so Wolflock can apologise." Mothy flashed a nonchalant smile to the grouchy crewman.

"O' course yah are..." Hognut sighed, cleaned his pipe and walked away.

Wolflock just stared after him in absolute astonishment.

"Can you tie a good knot?" Mothy asked, breaking his stunned trance.

"Saddles and good quality reins have buckles. So... I can't say I can." Normally Wolflock would have jumped at the chance to try something like this, but he just couldn't risk falling into the water at his own fault.

"Me either. I'll hold it here so you can get down. It should hold fast but I'll keep an eye on it just in case."

Mothy was in charge of his life? The boy who had lied to him so convincingly he hadn't been able to spot it? The boy who may be part of a terrible cult? His friend who may be part of a larger, more sinister plan? Wolflock drew back and went to refuse the offer but stopped himself. If he refused, it would show his hand. Mothy would instantly be informed that Wolflock had stopped trusting him and was still trying to discover his past. If Mothy was already aware of this, then he had helped Wolflock just now in order to set up this terrible 'accident'.

He scanned his eager friend. His shoulders were back, his smile seemed genuine, crinkling his eyes. He seemed excited, but relaxed. There had been no suspicious inflection to his words. Yet he had successfully deceived Wolflock before...

"Make sure you hold it tightly. I don't fancy a swim today."

"Of course I will. You're not wearing your bathers. If you fall in, I'll jump in to save you."

As Wolflock swung his leg over the railing he smiled. Deep down he believed it.

Why then was his gut wrenching at him to keep investigating?

He wrapped the rope around his wrist and leant back. His stomach dropped and his knees went weak. Wolflock gulped. He had done this before on trees and out of his bedroom when he'd been punished, but somehow the rock of the ship and the rushing water beneath him was unnerving. He was already here though, so there was no choice but to carry on. He gripped the rope and held his legs stiff, slowly walking backwards down the side of the pale ship toward the window he believed to be Dlumi's.

Thankfully, his calculations were correct. He could hear Dlumi yelling at someone through the door.

"I will not come out! You cannot make me! Leave me be!"

Wolflock felt a surge of daring. He bounced on the balls of his feet and jumped away from the ship, lowering himself and hurtling toward the window. He had miscalculated the length of rope he needed and expected to smack into the open window frame, but he felt the rope slip and he dropped half a foot right through the window.

Had Mothy let the rope slip deliberately? Did he know Wolflock was asking about him?

He had no time to think about it any longer as he shot through the window. He did not land gracefully.

He felt his legs hit the ground too hard and forced his torso forward, sending him into a painful roll, ending with Dlumi leaping out of the way and him hitting the door with a crunch.

"Wha-what!?" Dlumi gasped.

"I," Wolflock groaned and unwound himself from the door, rubbing his side as he got to his feet, "wanted to - ow, apologise to you."

"Oh, you are an awful man!" Dlumi bit her lip, her stormy grey eyes sparkling with tears.

Wolflock saw that her eyes were rubbed raw from wiping tears away and she spoke with a slightly blocked nose. He also noted the desk bin filled with roughly scrunched paper flooding out over the floor.

"Get out of my room or I'll throw you out of that window!"

Wolflock normally would have scoffed, but she grabbed his shirt and pulled him to the window. He was going to be thrown out into the river, have to swim to the edge and return home even more disgraced... Just like Dlumi was doing.

"Wait! I know you are different from your family!"

Dlumi stopped. Wolflock, who had raised his arm to block any incoming slaps, peeked through the gap in his fingers. caution etched her face.

"You... your family did not support your decisions. They tried to tell you to just stay home but you could not. You had bigger dreams, and you had to try. You had to chase your ambitions. You have a passion that won't rest, right? It gnaws at you until it's fulfilled? Like artists with their daemons, surely there must be daemons for ambitious people too."

If he could get her to see that they were similar, she would trust him. She'd accept his apology because they were the same in certain ways. At least... that's what he hoped.

Dlumi released his arm and huffed, sitting on the bed and gesturing for him to take a seat at the desk by waving her enormous hand. He dodged the wave which may have actually sent him back through the window and took a seat.

"How do you know these things?" She sighed, her

whole body heaving up and down.

"Because I left home for my ambitions too. No one in Plugh supported my investigative techniques-"

"I wonder why?" She shot a dark look at him.

"-But I couldn't stop. I couldn't let the truth not be known. I couldn't let justice go unserved. It was too important to give people the whole truth and clear their ignorance. But I don't believe I had the whole truth with you, and I am sorry for that. I feel I've very nearly lied about you through my harsh words."

"What do you mean?" Dlumi asked as she looked up in earnest.

"I said that you were like other Central Shiriling folk. That you were dull and poorly educated. I now know I should have changed that. No one is educated without experience. You wanted to be a businesswoman and you just couldn't get adequate training in Central Shiriling. That is not your fault. You were courageous and stepped out to seek it. People know Mystentine is a good place to build businesses, but the best have already been established for hundreds of years. Next to that geographically, Plugh is fair, but who really wants to go there?"

"No one wants to go there because there is said to

be black sheep that will eat you like lions and vampires that rule the town!" Dlumi interjected with wide eyes.

Wolflock stopped. Is that really what people thought of Plugh? Not that the people were awful, rude and controlling?

"There certainly are carnivorous sheep creatures. They're fairly docile though. They normally eat carrion. Their wool makes fantastic fabric though. Very waterproof, mostly dirt proof and weavers can make the fabric finer than normal wool."

The storm clouds in Dlumi's eyes seemed to part as her eyes lit up with fascination.

"And as for the vampires, they have their own sect that they mostly govern. They've had arrangements with the local human government for hundreds of years and I'd say there were fewer vampire attacks than human attacks. What is your hometown like?"

Dlumi's lips pressed as if she couldn't say what she really wanted to.

"It was fine."

"Was fine?"

"Corsh is so boring!" She burst out, gripping the sides of the bed. "It's all gem tree lumberjacks, ice apple farmers and carpenters! The only art is from the blacksmith and, even then, it's only woven metal. There is no time to read because we're always working, and no one wants to improve their farming skills by reading or researching. 'Everything is as it should be, Dlumi.' 'Don't go getting ideas, Dlumi.' "Why would you want to change a good thing, Dlumi?" We just don't do things that way here, Dlumi.' It drives me crazy!"

"No time to read? Are they mad? Who would not want to utilise the advances other people have developed?" Wolflock didn't even have to pretend it shocked him.

"They all told me I'd fail... They told me this was a fool's errand and I would be back within the year. They didn't give me any help or any extra money for the journey... They're lucky they didn't. I would have lost that too... I knew I'd fail but I had to at least try."

Wolflock frowned, uncomfortable with the self-pity presented before him. Instead of his mental web, he had an image of Dlumi putting a book together. It was common across Puinteyle for people to write Grimoires. Books filled with lessons they had learned over their lifetime that they wanted to be passed down. Recipes, spells, family mottos and other bits of useful information were often passed down through generations because of these books. Dlumi had begun to fill hers without even realising.

The wooden covers being folded with tanned leather and the pages being each sewn in were the lessons she had built upon. He could see her metaphorically writing with a quill as neatly as she could, trying to explain her lessons to those she loved. Wolflock could see though, Dlumi had quickly written in her book and, when it wasn't satisfactory, she had torn out the pages and sulked. He knew what he needed to do to fix this.

She needed to review those pages, see her mistakes, and learn from them.

And he knew just the person to do it.

"My father always said that every setback was merely a lesson. If you learned your mistake, then you would not need to pay for the lesson again."

"What do you mean?"

"Where did things go wrong?"

"When I left home..."

Wolflock clapped his hands loudly between their faces, startling her out of her stupor.

"No. That was the best thing you could have done. Where did you first go wrong in all seriousness?"

Dlumi thought for a moment. "When I gave fifty

coins to the blacksmith to buy jewels for the jewellery I had commissioned."

"And why?"

"Because he may have been a good blacksmith, but he was not a jeweler. They weren't fake, but they were terrible quality gems. Most of them shattered when they were being set into the pieces."

"So, you paid the blacksmith well for the lesson of asking the right people for the right information."

"I... I guess so?"

"And your next mistake?"

They went on and on, going back through Dlumi's entire venture, taking her mistakes and reforming each into lessons. Dlumi's whole demeanour changed from being a victim of circumstance to being proud she had learned so much. Wolflock had no business experience himself, nor did he have much interest in business, but his father and tutors had trained him to manage an estate and these questions were precisely the ones his father had trained him in, so that each year the estate was protected and thrived.

"When you go home to your family, tell them you paid for lessons in business and you did everything you could. They may still not understand, but you'll know in your heart, with all truth and sincerity, that you're more prepared next time."

Dlumi looked hopeful for a moment, smiling and nodding. Her posture was relaxed and her eyes thoughtful, but then she slumped again, sighing.

"But after selling all the jewellery I have nothing left. I don't know what else to do."

"What does Central Shiriling have in abundance that you haven't seen anywhere else?"

"Pff. Ice," she scoffed. "Ice and snow. There's nothing there, really. Maybe ice apples."

An idea burst like lightning in Wolflock's mind, illuminating its elements so quickly he had to say it out loud, so they weren't lost.

"Ice! You could ship ice!"

"Huh?"

"No, I mean it. No one in all of Puinteyle has ice. You know how well it keeps meat and vegetables, and it makes drinks delicious in Summer! If you could learn how to ship ice to other countries, you wouldn't even have to leave home."

"You can't ship ice, Wolflock. It melts too quickly."

"But what if you could? Listen, I'm not a businessman, but Froderyk is. Speak to him about getting a deal with some of the wizards and scientists at Mystentine. They do all sorts of experiments there. Maybe don't even go home for long. Get work in Mystentine, study business and help fund research into transporting ice to other regions."

Dlumi nodded, thinking carefully. "My family already thinks I'm crazy, so there's no harm in trying."

"I've heard people say it's all about who you know. If you don't have anything to offer a scientist yet for their efforts, then maybe offer them a portion of the proceeds when things get rolling."

Dlumi nodded faster. "That actually sounds brilliant. You are quite clever, aren't you?"

Wolflock smiled coyly. "What can I say? I have a gift."

"You're frightened of having to go home too, you said?"

"Aye..." he replied with a small sigh.

"Even if you do, it will be ok. But I doubt Mothy would let either of you fail. He's a clever boy too. You two could work with me in Mystentine until the term starts up again if you wanted."

For the first time since he had initially worried about missing the safe period to ascend the mountain to

Mystentine University, Wolflock felt an odd cushion of safety in Dlumi's words. Her unwarranted kindness wasn't desired, but it made him feel something... odd. Like someone else having his back made life that little easier.

"Thank you, Dlumi. I appreciate that. How did you and Mothy meet?"

He had brought her around to a stage where redirecting the conversation was easy. He'd get what he needed to hear. Maybe Dlumi would even know Mothy's middle name and he'd be saved from his extended punishment.

"I met Mothy when I first boarded the ship. You were right earlier. I traveled to Shellinden and then further up the river towards Corl, but my rental burnt down. I'm so used to stone houses that I left the lantern going. It was such a stupid mistake." She gave a mournful sigh. "I travelled back to Shellinden with what was left because it was cheaper to do a few weeks of labour on the ship than to rent anywhere else until it met me further up the river.

Mothy was waved off by a handsome Uluken man and a pretty Shellinmerth woman. They acted as if he was their son or younger brother. He came on with that one big bag and that was it. Even I had a trunk and two bags, and I consider myself a low maintenance person."

"Did he ever unpack it?"

"I didn't pay much attention but, from what I've seen of his room, it's always been left exactly as he found it."

"He's an odd one." Wolflock nodded to himself.

"You can say that again."

"Oh? Did you see him do something strange?" Was this it? Was Dlumi about to tell him the information he sought after?

"Well.... Sort of. We collected a few new passengers when we got to Allunare. One of them was one of those Troston priests. You know? Tall, bald on the top, dark robes with red trim. He wore one of the domed crosses. I mean... there was nothing wrong with the man. He joined us for meals, spoke politely to anyone who addressed him and was pleasant enough. He did a couple of strange things of course, as they do. He prayed over his food until it went cold, he wouldn't touch any women and he always tried to find answers to tricky questions in that big book they carry on their belts. He was by no means a bad man though."

"What did that have to do with Mothy?"

"Well, the moment Mothy saw him, he hid. It was the first time I'd seen him stop smiling. When we all boarded together at Shellinden, Mothy was the only person to try to help me out of my mood. He was kind, brought me food and kept me company. He was bright and entertaining. When this priest came on board, Mothy was nowhere to be seen, though. I found him even hiding in his own cupboard. He yelled out 'boo!' but I knew in my gut that he wasn't wanting to be found."

"Did Mothy know the man? The priest?" Wolflock leaned forward eagerly.

"By his behaviour, you'd think so. But the priest had come from Western Shellinmerth. Born and bred there. He was only coming across into Quarenth because there was a special meeting or something in Chaysaile. I was worried about Mothy not eating, so I asked the old man if he knew Mothy. My question completely bewildered him. That's how I knew where he was from and where he was going. He was on for about a fortnight until we got to Warpa, just inside the Quarenth border. Like I said, he was an odd man but not a liar. I have learned very well to spot liars."

"Now that kind of skill will save your business." Wolflock plastered a smile across his face as he felt more threads of Mothy's mystery coming together.

Mothy had clear connections with the Troston church. The symbol. The burn. The reaction to the priest. Was he running from them? Was he part of the evil branches of the faith?

"How did you first get to know Mothy?" Dlumi broke into his thoughts with a particularly melodic voice that Wolflock had just picked up on.

"When I first arrived, and the ship was under lockdown due to the Captain's illness, Mothy stopped me from getting in trouble and rushing out onto the deck to watch the launch. He tripped me on the stairs and we snuck up to the crow's nest. I feel we've been good friends ever since."

Dlumi giggled. "Good friends? You two are like brothers. I've not seen Mothy take to any individual on the ship like he has with you. Even when you two aren't together he talks about what you've both been talking about. Lockie this and Lockie that. It's adorable."

"Really? I... I wasn't aware."

"You're the same though. Whenever Mothy isn't around, even when you come to apologise to someone, you keep drawing the conversation back to him. Your friendship is beautiful."

"Thank you, Dlumi."

"No, thank you. I feel much better now. As I said though, if either of you find yourselves in trouble in Shiriling, just send me a letter. I'll do whatever I can to help."

"Actually, I did have a question. Do you know Mothy's full name?"

Dlumi thought for a moment and giggled. "Now that I think about it, I've never heard anyone address him as anything but 'Mothy'. Why do you ask?"

"Just a game we're playing. It's nothing."

Wolflock nodded once, shook her hand, and promptly found himself pulled into a rib-cracking bear hug by the gigantic muscled woman.

"Ack! Thanks!" He strained, hobbling off when she put him down. As he left the cabin, he felt an uncomfortable crunch under his foot. He'd stepped on the cold tea he'd brought earlier as a peace offering. "Ugh..."

"See you at dinner, Mr Felen!" she called out after him as he retreated to his room for a moment to recuperate.

Groaning, sporting what he thought was certainly a broken rib, he began to wonder. Was Mothy investigating him back? Had he been on Mothy's radar this whole time? Were they friends? Mothy had been associated with the Troston church in some way, but how? It must have been such a scarring experience that even the mere appearance of a priest had sent him into hiding... unless Mothy himself had done something so horrific that being spied by even an average priest would put his life in jeopardy.

There was only one other known person on the ship who knew his middle name. Only one person who knew more about Mothy than Dlumi and Froderyk. One person who could give Wolflock the answers he needed. Ungul.

Rhiannon D. Elton

CHAPTER 7

The Nobles

He knew she of all people wouldn't give him the information he needed. She wanted to see him punished... Wolflock sat up and realised the sensation of dread no longer surrounded having to work like a packhorse for a month. It didn't mean as much to him as finding out what Mothy's history was and why he was hiding it. He had to know the answers.

Wolflock looked out of his round window, seeing the dark shadows of the mid-afternoon darken the mixed pine and deciduous trees. The closer they came to the Dragon's Spine mountain range, the more the world prepared for a constant sprinkling of ice and snow. Judging by the shadows, Wolflock had only a few hours left to speak to Ungul and Uhnha before the Captain came to dinner. The likelihood of him being able to ask any questions in regard to Mothy while he was breaking his back working on the ship was miniscule. He had to get the answers now. Even if it didn't save him from punishment.

The ladies weren't in their cabin, but Wolflock knew they preferred to be out on deck. They often sat at the very bow of the ship, the wind blowing through their thick black hair. As he came on deck, it was exactly as he envisioned. Ungul sat on the left, Uhnha sat on the right, both staring forward and taking no heed of him as he approached them with trepidation.

Neither wore shoes and their attire was significantly different from one another. Uhnha wore a bright orange striped skirt that sat low on her hips and a finely woven shawl with cascading aquamarine beads. Pink slashes ran across her hips and, like her sister, she never smiled, but instead often looked despondent. Her hair was free and sat around her head like a black pompom, often shrouding her face with a mere turn of her head. She rolled a salt stone bracelet around her wrist whenever she thought Ungul wasn't looking, each bead was carved into a perfect sphere except one, which was carved into a swaddled infant.

Ungul wore no jewellery besides a half disc necklace and white beads in her hair. Her breasts were bound tightly to her chest by two crossing white sashes with a black zigzag pattern and her dusky yellow skirt was bound between her legs to make them into pants. Wolflock had only seen Myna tie her dress like that when she wanted to prove a point to the local boys that she could do anything they could do and still be a lady about it.

Both of their bodies rippled with the muscles of warriors and they stood a good foot taller than Wolflock, drawing a tinge of fear from the pit of his gut. He swallowed it back down and clenched his fists. He could do this. He had to.

He had seen Froderyk respond to hearing that someone worked hard. Fuhji wanted to nurture others, and Dlumi had softened with knowing someone wanted to help her and not just tell her she was wasting her time.

Ungul and Uhnha were closed off from most social interactions between the crew and company, as if they had such a particularly dark secret hidden that even a little conversation would reveal them. Wolflock didn't know enough about the Blickland Forest folk politics or culture to even guess if they had a distinction of nobility or markings of a trade. The Blickland Forest was filled with secrets. The people rarely ventured from their forest, believing the trees showed them where they could go and where their limits should be. They were known to be the best spiritual and physical healers, but they kept their medicines in the strictest confidence. They wanted for very little outside the forest and protected it with fierce devotion. That was all he knew, though. They didn't mingle in external politics unless it affected their forest and their ambassadors scouted for miles around the forest to ensure no outside forces could creep in or disturb their balance.

While they didn't spy him, Wolflock watched them both.

Uhnha's shoulders slumped, and she shook occasionally as if she'd begin to cry again. She spent most days crying with a forlorn stare into nothingness.

Ungul, on the other hand, remained stoic and taciturn. She shoulders were always squared, and her jaw set to stop any conversation directly at her. Ungul knew the answers Wolflock required though. She stood, walked and spoke as a duty-bound warrior. A soldier.

Duty... Wolflock thought to himself. Duty to

family and honour...

"How do you do it?" he asked, causing Uhnha to jump and Ungul to whip her head around to face him.

"What do you want now?" Ungul's wide nose wrinkled into a snarl.

"How do you dedicate your life to your family's honour? I... I've given up on Mothy's middle name for now. I have asked everyone, and no one knows except for you and Mothy. Neither of you will reveal it, so there is no point. I'd rather understand you better instead. Even if I am forced to work for a month, the lessons I've learned from the others are enough to compensate for the discomfort. You both are the only ones I..." he swallowed again and struggled to keep eye contact with those dark pits in Ungul's eyes, threatening to engulf him if one more insult was even suspected, "I haven't yet apologised too."

The ebony-skinned ladies both stayed silent. Their eyes bored into him like drills.

"I'm... sorry for offending you both. I'm sorry for revealing your secrets to the entire ship without so much as even speaking to you first. I'm sorry for my lack of tact, delicacy, and I'm very sorry if you feel I've dishonoured you."

There was no motion in either of them until the

words 'dishonoured you' arose. Uhnha's eyelids dropped and her thick lips pursed for a moment, whereas Ungul tilted her head a fraction to the left. Not the response he was thinking he would get.

"I think... I think I can relate to both of you. See... Uhnha, I too feel trapped and my own feelings disregarded by my family."

"I did not say that," Uhnha frowned and shook her head fearfully as Ungul turned her face, filled with concern.

"You didn't have to. You show tiny signs that I've trained myself to pick up on that showed me you don't like the mention of dishonour. You have an unspoken contempt for it, which I completely understand. Where I'm from, social graces get you much further than real skills or kindness. It's all about who you know and who you kiss the shoes of. It's sickening. You probably felt as suffocated as me and acted out, yes? This man, who treated you so abominably as to lead you on and take advantage of you, offered you the excitement and freedom you craved. Just as seeing through people's facades and observing the truth of the details does for me."

Uhnha sighed and her shoulders rose as she looked to her sister. "He is not wrong. He hasn't been wrong at all."

Wolflock had thought this entire time that Uhnha was the frightened one. That she was the weaker sibling, but, as she looked defiantly up into her sister's strong eyes, he saw an inner fire. That was why Ungul guarded her so vigilantly. Ungul was desperately trying to placate their parents, their honour and their family name, but Uhnha was trying to placate her soul.

"Are you frightened she'll run the first chance she gets?"

Ungul's eyes flashed at him, filled with lethal warning.

"Uhnha? Do you believe she's dragging you home to do things you don't want to do? To be trapped again?"

Uhnha blinked. The smaller woman squared herself up to her sister. Just that small tilt of the shoulders made her look far less small and more like an agile panther cat, ready to leap. Ungul was more like a bull.

"This is none of your business, boy," Ungul hissed.

"It is, actually. This disturbance between you and your sister has made your mood so defensive and cold that it has hurt Mothy and it is my duty to my friend to rectify the situation."

Ungul stopped snarling and looked taken

very aback.

"But you're only doing this to decrease your punishment."

"No. Not anymore. I'm doing this because I need to know that my dear friend is not a fiend and is the person I believe he is. I need to get to the bottom of this, so that there is no question in my mind that he is a good person. If I have to work on the ship for six months, it will be worth it to know that again. You need not tell me his name, but you need to listen to me in order to make amends with your sister and cease this stupid, unkind behaviour."

Wolflock held his chin high and his shoulders back with a strength and boldness that caused Ungul to grit her teeth in fury once more.

"You don't know anything! You have no honour or duty to your-"

"I have more honour than you!" Wolflock shouted back. "I come from the ancient Felen line and I was banished from my home because I would not dishonour myself or my town with disgusting disregard for the integrity of my fellows. Family means more to me than you'll ever know and I would stand by my sister in the face of all politics, no matter what choice she made. If it was in her best interest, I would always be at her back. I certainly wouldn't keep her as a prisoner for my family's wishes."

Ungul flinched.

"That being said," his tone softened and his body trembled with adrenaline. "I would hope that she would listen to me before she made impulsive mistakes. But those are her lessons to learn. As are mine."

"He's wiser than Ata." Uhnha heaved a frustrated sigh.

Ungul punched the railing. "In a stupid, annoying, rude way."

Wolflock had expected that punch to meet his face.

"You wield such power, Ungul," he continued, holding his breath. "I remember my sister tying her skirt like yours only when she needed to exert her most extreme power. Myna hates moving at the best of times, but she will never let a slight to herself go unchallenged, even if it means going to intense measures. You're perceptive and intelligent, but you guard yourself unnecessarily. What reason could you have for not sharing your concerns with your sister? As a noble woman, have you not been trained in negotiations?"

Ungul and Uhnha looked at each other with a

knowing glance.

"It's... it's not how the Kifalme family do things. We have a strict code of honour and family above the individual."

"And how is that working for you?" Wolflock scoffed. Tradition that remained untested and unquestioned was something he couldn't stand. "Wait... Did you say Kifalme?"

The ladies stayed silent.

The Kifalme family were said to have ancient blood from the very forest itself and were charged to be the guardians of the forest. If their line ended, the forest was said to die with them.

"The Kifalme? The old royal family? One of the oldest and strongest families in the Blickland Forest?"

"Some would say in all Syongdelen." Ungul bristled with pride.

"I understand now. Uhnha believes you're taking her back only to restore the family name and that you feel disgraced by her actions. She doesn't feel like you were worried about her wellbeing at all."

"Uhnha..." Ungul's face showed the concern she displayed every time Uhnha wasn't looking. "Uhnha, he is not right is he? You know I came to make sure you were safe. You know I take you back because you are not well. You need to recover."

Uhnha's eyes swelled with tears and she looked away.

"You take me back because our parents sent you to."

"No! No, I defied them to come and get you! Mothy knows this. He wouldn't tell me where you were until I swore to him you would be cared for. You really thought this was all because I didn't want to see our family name seen poorly? I thought that not talking to anyone and keeping us away from the others would help. Only Captain and Mothy know anything... And now this boy too. That was how I protected the family name. Everything else was only to protect you."

"Why force me to come back then?" Uhnha pleaded.

"You've been through so much. You know only our healers will understand and be able to help you heal. It would give you time to discuss your grievances with our parents. I'd be able to help you find a way to be happy that wouldn't hurt your relationship with the elders. I couldn't bear to see you exiled for something so fickle as a lover."

"Why didn't you say any of this?" Tears streamed

down Uhnha's face as she shook her hands in exasperation. "I thought you were dragging me back to stop political disgrace! That you'd give me back to mama and ta and be done with it!"

"No! You thought that all this time? You didn't think I was standing by you all along? I thought you were grieving, and you did not want to talk about it." Ungul took her sister's arms and squeezed her.

Wolflock just stood back and watched them. He thought Plugians were awful at communicating. The Blickland sisters' discourse just showed him it was universal.

Both women hugged, cried and began talking quickly in their native language, filled with clicks and soothing noises. Wolflock had little choice but to stand there and let them finish. Minutes passed. Then half an hour. Then an hour. The sun sat on the trees to the East, lazily dipping down into the blanket of the horizon.

"How did you know we did not understand one another?" Ungul finally said to him, breaking him from his admiration of the sunset.

"Huh? Oh. I have a little sister. We always have the faces you two did. We learned quickly to recognise it and resolve our issues because... well... we didn't have friends. I mean... Myna did. Sometimes. She gets into a lot of drama and her friendship circle changes too regularly. But without each other to rely on we had no one. Being different means most people want to see you fail because they're jealous you have the strength to stand out. It's easier and lazier to be jealous than it is to rise to the occasion."

"Are you going to do that with Mothy?" Uhnha asked.

Wolflock's brow furrowed. "What do you mean?"

Ungul had turned her eyes away as he spoke.

"You two are arguing, aren't you?"

"Whatever gave you that impression?"

Uhnha looked to her sister and back to Wolflock.

"He... Ungul, you told me he said he-"

"Well, this boy had shown himself to be nothing but a rude little upstart and I wasn't having a bar of it. I wasn't going to let Mothy be hurt by him!" Ungul cried, waving her hand in a wide motion to Wolflock.

"Did... did you say something to Mothy? About me?" He was perplexed. Had Ungul tried to harm his friendship?

"I told him the truth. He came to me, upset that I'd asked you to find his middle name. I saw you talking to Miss Korsaki and her partner, then swinging down to

Dlumi's room. I could only assume you were still hunting for answers. I gave Mothy a little scare when I approached him as he held your rope and I told him what you were doing and how you'd lied to him. You weren't doing any of this to make amends, but just to avoid punishment. It... it upset him a bit, but you had been so unlike him and I didn't want you to taint him. We have known him so well and..."

Wolflock couldn't see auras without the assistance of a device to look through, but by Ungul's ashamed gaze he realised that she had been jealous of Mothy's affection towards him.

"You don't know his middle name, do you?"

"I do, actually," she said with a sigh of defeat. "But he didn't give it to me. Had you kept making friends on board, he may very well have trusted you with it. Something he did not trust me with."

"I don't want to know his middle name. But I do want to know why you believe your relationship with him is so strong and why you'd want to stop him from being my friend." Wolflock sat on the railing next to Uhnha, staring into her eyes adamantly.

"You said you wanted to know for sure that your friend was not a 'fiend'. I can assure you that he is not.

Even after all the horrors, he must have endured, he is the purest soul I have ever seen. This all began when I reached Shellinden.

"I had been tracking Uhnha for many months and it had not been hard to do. A Syongdelen woman dressed in our family's clothes stands out. When I reached the big city, I lost her. There is so much fashion, so many people of all shapes, sizes, colours and abilities. It was like finding a single mite on a panther. Cold, alone and unable to find a room to stay in because of the Beltaine celebrations, I went to rest by the docks. Although many people go there, it was not so bad because the breeze was fresh. That's when Mothy found me.

"Are you ok, ma'am?' he asked with that bright smile. 'I know somewhere you can sleep if you would like to come out of the night.'

"His innocence and kindness wounded me and I began to cry like a baby. I told him everything. He had seen Uhnha and said that he knew everyone in Eastern Shellinden. I begged him to take me to her, but he insisted that I rest for the night. That evening he went to see her himself and ask her questions about me."

"I had only asked if you were mad. When he believed you weren't mad, he let you come to collect me from the hospital." Uhnha responded calmly.

"She had already lost the baby and received compensation from the man's family. She was ready to get away from him now. This all took a few days of back and forth to organise. This gave me time to see the merchant cart that Mothy's guardian, Hazzim, ran. Mothy was so friendly to everyone. He was a hard worker and his charity knew no bounds. Hazzim encouraged it to Mothy's delight. Everything in the whole world left the sheltered boy in awe. I'd never met such a creature.

"Finally, the day came when I was to see Uhnha for myself. We walked through the streets of Shellinden and Mothy gave me a strange tour of where he'd climbed to the top of buildings and what he'd eaten when he sat there, as well as what the sunset or sunrise looked like from those places. He is an odd, yet enchanting, little boy. But then something happened.

"There was a Troston procession through the streets. I'd never seen one before. All these people in black robes, trimmed with red with their hoods up. They cross their hands together, like they're begging for meals off the street, and they whisper their holy words like demons trying to drive someone insane. Mothy froze and went pale. The breeze picked up and a gust of wind blew their hoods back. The boy went from white to red like a firestorm.

"I'd seen that face before on my warriors. If one of their family or troop had been killed by a creature, and if they ever saw it again, they would go into a reckless frenzy as if they couldn't control themselves. Mothy was doing just that.

"He charged forward and thrashed like a wildcat when I caught him around his middle. His face looked like he was going to explode.

"'Let me go! I'll kill her! I'll kill her!' was all I could make out. He was babbling and foaming, throwing himself around desperately trying to break free, but I would not let him. So young and so kind, but, as he saw those Trostons pass and deflated in my arms, I realised he was not innocent. He stayed silent and blank-faced for hours after that. I saw Uhnha and was offered a room with her in the hospital, but I took Mothy home first and told Hazzim what had happened. We came back the next day to see how he was doing but he hadn't emerged. The next day was the same. And the next.

"Finally, four days later Mothy sent us word that he was going to board a ship to go to Mystentine University, but we could also board in order to get back home as quickly as possible. We came to visit at that note and Mothy was cheerful, bright and bubbly again.

"Hazzim explained a little bit about how he and Mothy met, but, at one stage he sighed, bringing Mothy into a paternal embrace.

"'You learn all you can, my young Mothy Meldryk Enitnelav. When you are finished there will be a home for you in Uluken near Hanan.'

"Mothy flinched.

"'You know what, Hazzim? I'm going to leave that old name behind. I don't need it anymore. I'll never go by that again. I'll just be Mothy Enitnelav.'

"He had seemed so proud to be making this decision. It wasn't until after we reached the day before we boarded the Silver Ice Hair that I found out Meldryk means-"

"From the powerful mill," Mothy interjected shortly.

The three of them turned to see Mothy smiling at them, but his eyes were wide, making the smile look deranged and wild. The sun had set and the ship's lanterns had been lit, giving his face an eerie glow.

"Meldryk is the name of a family who lived outside of Vasor in Chalongesh."

"Mothy, I-"

Mothy raised his hand as Ungul tried to speak.

"I don't go by that name anymore. I hope you don't have to work anymore, Wolflock. I'm going to bed." He raised his hand, touched the tip of his ear, and then pressed it out to them in an attempt at a wave that looked more like he was trying to deflect someone from hitting him.

His voice cracked at the height of his sentence and Wolflock winced as he used his proper name. He was truly upset. Wolflock had to make him understand though. He had to let him know that he just needed to know him better. He had to see how he'd ended up here without any lies.

Mothy began to run off and Wolflock sprinted after him.

That was it. All the pieces had a place. Each ring of Wolflock's mental web had connected. The fine strands of Froderyk, Fuhji, Dlumi, Ungul and Uhnha were now connected with all the clues he needed to fill out all but a few details of Mothy's past. The name 'Meldryk' had sealed it all together, but the final piece that stuck all the loose bits of web to where they were meant to be... The action Mothy performed when he lied. It made sense now.

He raised his hand to his head whenever he lied. Just that piece of evidence along with the name 'Meldryk' made everything clear. Wolflock took off after Mothy with all the times he had touched his ear or played with his hair mid-conversation. Each piece made Wolflock's web of clues so much clearer.

He had been so plagued with thinking that Mothy was some kind of conspirator or secretly an evil being running from their wrongdoings because he so desperately wanted it to be a lie. He realised now that he had dug so hard to find the information in order to prove himself wrong. He hadn't let the idea that Mothy was truly a victim creep into his mind either. He couldn't afford that doubt to taint his investigation due to his own bias. Now he knew it. Now he knew he had to speak to Mothy. He couldn't let it go on any longer.

As he caught up to his friend and grabbed his hand, Mothy turned sharply, a look of fear and sadness splashed over his face, his eyes glittering with tears. Wolflock continued to move forward and pulled him into a hug.

"I have something I need to tell you."

Mothy stiffened with alarm but followed Wolflock as he led him down into the hull and to the secret box room. Wolflock took a few deep breaths and began as Mothy wiped his eyes.

"I know you have heard me asking after you. I know you don't like that. You're scared I'll find your secrets and reveal them to everyone. But I need to tell you something of the utmost importance. Something I've never told anyone. Not even Myna or my father."

"What is it?" Mothy's tearful expression transformed into concern.

Wolflock took another deep, slow breath.

"I need to tell you about how I was the one who was responsible for the disappearance of my mother."

Rhiannon D. Elton

CHAPTER 8

The Greatest Crime

What?"

"I don't want anyone else to hear. Come on."

Wolflock lead Mothy down into the crew's quarters, the hammocks swinging silently with the sway of the ship, then down again into the hull.

"Do you want to go back in the box?" Mothy asked with a subtle sniff as he wiped his eyes.

Wolflock tried to think of something sharp and witty to retort to, the whole world of box pun humour open to him, but Mothy's teary sincerity weakened him.

"Yes," was all he could manage.

They crawled into the space, but not before

Wolflock grabbed a fairy dust lantern from the hook by the stairs.

"Don't want to catch on fire again. That would be terrible."

Mothy didn't laugh. He just pulled his knees to his chest and refused to make eye contact.

"Listen..." Wolflock began steadily. "I didn't mean to upset you in my search for answers. I just needed to know."

Mothy took in a deep breath and slowly exhaled, raising his gaze.

"You know the name Meldryk, aye?"

Wolflock nodded. "Everyone does."

"You know what they did then?"

"Not all of it. It was fairly significant news throughout all of Eastern and Central Puinteyle, but news can be inaccurate."

Mothy nodded slowly and released his legs, huffing out a breath and letting his shoulders drop.

"I didn't know what Meldryk meant until I was with Hazzim. It means 'from the powerful mill'. Being from a powerful mill didn't seem so bad... until I realised what they were milling."

"I've only heard rumours," Wolflock frowned

wearily.

"My Ma gave me the Meldryk name before it all went bad. I mean... it was always bad. But she thought it would give me a chance to find my way home if I was ever taken from her."

Wolflock grimaced. "You're a slave?"

Mothy snorted. "No. I mean... I was. Technically. But I was never really a slave in my mind. Ma always said I didn't have the heart of a slave." His demeanour changed. "Alright, Lockie. You got me here and you know my full name. I'll fill you in on the rest-"

"Hold up a minute, my friend!" Wolflock raised his hand. "I said I'd tell you about my misfortune. You'll have to wait your turn if you suddenly feel like sharing."

Mothy pulled back and cocked his head to the side. After a moment, he waved his hand grandiosely between them.

"Well then. By all means, go ahead, oh tormented one."

They both snorted with laughter but, as it settled, the silence felt tense.

"She... I was... it was..." Wolflock felt his chest constricting as it saw it in his mind's eye.

Mothy stayed silent, but he leaned forward as if to

comfort his friend.

"I was five. Myna was only two, so she doesn't remember anything, thankfully. Towards the end of the war, Plugh was attacked in a savage assault. Of course, the past queen's assassinators collaborated with the Trostons and cut as many deals with them as they could. Everyone knows that. Something about being in the new world or creating it or some rubbish."

"When I was in Shellinden, I found out that there was the main branch of perfectly normal Trostons, who stuck to themselves, but most of the other offshoots had terrible agendas stemming back to the time of the Evil King. Most people think that it's the offshoots that made deals and still think they can be upheld," Mothy offered nonchalantly.

Wolflock frowned in thought and continued, "Well one of those deals in Grothener was that they could steal people to make into slaves from whatever towns they tried to destroy. Plugh was lucky to be saved by the Draconians. Our old house is a little way away from Plugh, so the Trostons raided us for hours before we were rescued... My father had heard the horses and servants shouting and woken up my mother to make sure that my sister and I were safe. He went to the armoury and grabbed our family's sword to defend us. Mother got me first. I can just remember her telling me to stay silent as we could hear men downstairs in the parlour, smashing things and shouting..."

Mother had pulled me down the hall as quickly as possible, past the library and into a cupboard as we saw shadows of men passing through the dark hall. We waited, quivering like leaves in a storm. She held me so tightly I thought she'd crush me as we listened to the men smash through the door beside the very cupboard we were hiding in. Mother peeked out of the crack in the door and then grabbed my arm, making a final run for Myna's room. We made it just as the men down the hall burst out of the room they had finished searching. I just remember how my arm ached when she finally set me free from her vice grip."

Wolflock rubbed his arm unconsciously as if it still hurt.

"Myna's room was a mess. It was a rather large room with soft toys and pillows scattered everywhere, as well as half our library. I remember it all as if it were yesterday. There was a central crib, and the room was a customary soft blue for girls, but it was hard to see because of the paint that had been thrown at it. Myna thought herself an artist in her infancy. Had we not known that Myna was a very messy child, we would have thought she had already been taken. But she was sleeping soundly in a large mound of cushions beside her crib. Only my sister could sleep through such turmoil.

"'Quickly!' Mother breathed and picked up Myna, who was still oblivious to the danger we were in. 'Wolflock! Unlock the cupboard!'

"I did as I was told without hesitation and we began hearing the door to the room being banged upon by the intruders. Mother's sharp blue eyes were as wide as they could go. I'd never seen her so frightened. She pushed us into the cupboard and motioned with a finger to her shaking lips for us to be silent. She began feeling the back wall of the old cupboard until she found a small latch, which I pressed for her, but it made a loud creaking noise and the men coming into the room fell silent.

I peered through the thin slit between the doors and saw five men in long black dirty cloaks, listening intently. They had long hoods that stood up straight and menacingly. I thought at the time that they were trying to mimic witch and wizard hats without the practical large brim. On the front of their robes, they had a red cross with an arch touching the three shorter branches. Just like the one on your back but without the added bits.

"'Check the room! Those fire breathing devils will be here soon,' one of them growled, and the others scattered through the room, tearing it apart.

"Mother was holding Myna still so she motioned for me to open the secret compartment very carefully and slowly, so it wouldn't make a noise. I... If I'd just been better..."

Wolflock's voice trembled as his throat clenched. He couldn't look Mothy in the eye. Accounting the tale was hard enough.

"I opened the back of the cupboard a little more and it creaked so loudly. The nearest ruffian heard the noise and came to investigate the cupboard, which sent Mother into a panic. She ripped the door open, not caring for how loud it was and shoved both of us inside before they could realise what was happening.

"'Stay silent! I love you,' she sobbed as she forced the hidden door closed.

"I only remembered hearing her scream as the men grabbed her and gloated. I tried to push the door open again but I couldn't. I couldn't open the door from inside, and my sister and I cried as we heard Mother battle against her captors, thrashing around and knocking over the crib and much of the other furniture. Finally, we heard a tremendous roar that shook the whole house and Myna's window was smashed in from the tail of a dragon who had landed on our roof.

"'Godspeed, you fools!' one shouted after the dragon's roar ended.

I heard a terrible thud and Mother groaned and then a battle ensued outside...

"We waited for hours, unable to get out of the secret space in the cupboard until our father and one of the King's officials saved us. Father has never laughed... never smiled... since Myna and I were the only ones to emerge that day... My mother was his light and joy and if he hadn't been injured defending us, he would be out there looking for her. Because of his leg, he can only send his employees out after her. After that night he moved us to the house I grew up in, which was right in town and well protected."

Wolflock held his head high and set his jaw against the tears that had prickled in his piercing blue eyes. Mothy moved to sit beside him, putting a supportive arm around his shoulders and smiling kindly.

"How are you feeling?"

"Honestly? Terrible. Like a wound that's been

festering for a while just got cleaned. But I feel better for it."

Mothy breathed a laugh out of his nose and nodded.

"I guess it's my turn then. You know... to feel clean... er. I did wash this morning mind you."

Wolflock smiled.

"How did you know though? Before I start. How did you figure it all out? I thought I was good at keeping my own secrets."

"You are," Wolflock nodded in admiration. "It took me ages to figure out what was truth and what wasn't. If I hadn't seen abused horses, I would have believed your scar was nothing. But I've seen brands before. Someone who has been branded so severely wouldn't have had a good childhood. Then asking the Captain if he was familiar with the symbol confirmed my theory. You had been somehow associated with a branch of the Trostons. I learned from Froderyk and Fuhji that you knew what runaways would do if they were being pursued. From Dlumi it was confirmed that you had terrible experiences with Trostons, most likely those who were higher in that particular faction given your response to the priest who was ferried before Corl."

Mothy smiled. "Yeah.... Dlumi found me in a

cupboard."

"Why a cupboard? Why not just your room?"

"Well... when someone is looking for you, they don't think to look in strange spaces like cupboards or even under beds. They think you'll just be visible in the room. It's a good way to get some sleep."

"Very well... odd... but very well." Wolflock scratched his chin.

Then he shrugged and continued, "Then, of course, there is the action you perform when you lie."

Mothy's eyebrows raised.

"Pardon?"

"You raise your hand to your face and head whenever you lie. When I thought back over it, I realised all the times you'd lied to me and what it meant. That tied together all but a few loose ends to my conclusions."

"And when did you think I lied?" Mothy folded his arms and leaned back with an air of confidence.

Wolflock mimicked him and began counting.

"Firstly, when you said you found this crate as it was. Clearly, from how Dlumi found you, this felt like a safe hiding place. Secondly, when you told me everything, I said about you was correct. I believe I got the flavour of it all correct, but the details were all wrong. Thirdly, you said you didn't see auras. You do. You probably weren't born with it, but heightened stress can bring on that ability."

"I still don't know what you mean by that, though," Mothy interrupted. "You mentioned Seers, which was another term they used at the mill for witches. They burned a few of the younger slaves at the stake for using magic and divination, so it's the kind of thing I wouldn't want to share around. They threatened me with the same if I didn't stop using herbs to help the other slaves. I figured I was some kind of witch too."

"Seeing auras can stem from trying to keep you safe," Wolflock explained. "Do you ever see light or colours around people?"

"Yeah. Just a little."

"That's what the royal family's seers do. Those colours are said to change when someone's emotional and spiritual state change. Some seers use it to strengthen their medicine and others use it to see through deception. I only know what is discussed in politics about it all."

Mothy nodded with a thoughtful smile. "Huh... I guess that makes sense. Alright. Carry on."

Wolflock cleared his throat and continued.

"Fourth, Autumn doesn't make you a bit tired. This

must be the time of year when something that left you with a particularly horrible memory occurred. Your facial expression when you said this time of year made you weary and your hand reaching above your shoulders made it clear to me that this date caused you pain to even think about it. I don't know what specifically, but I can imagine it is something severely terrible.

"Fifth, you have had to steal often in the past and no, you didn't call it borrowing. You're lucky I'm the only one who noticed this telling movement indicated your dishonesty. I don't believe anyone else would be as impartial."

Mothy just chuckled, shaking his head.

"Sixth, clearly the brand on your back is not a birthmark. And finally, you had no intention of going to bed just before."

Mothy half smiled, looking resigned.

"Don't fret though," Wolflock spoke again with a sincere expression. "I won't tell anyone else when you're lying. I promise. I believe you've enough life experience to know when to lie and I don't think it would be to my disadvantage or with malicious intent. You're not that kind of person."

"Judging by my name you wouldn't think that..."

Mothy responded darkly.

"Your middle name is... well, it's terrible. But that's your middle name. It's not who you are. It's a key from your mother. That's it."

Mothy sighed, clearly unconvinced.

"The Meldryk's were all convicted and sent to the Labyrinth Forest for their crimes. Everyone knows that. Their fervent and dangerously zealous obedience to their church leaders and the term 'lord' was another thing that gave you away."

"Huh?"

"When I told you that my father was technically a Lord, you said you'd never call me that. Yet you'd call me a Prince or a Duke. It cast the doubt I needed to not believe you would be like them."

"I should hope I'd never be thought of in the same box as them... But... Sometimes you have to be a monster to defeat monsters. Sometimes being kind and nice and... sometimes gentleness is weakness. I had to do terrible things to... You see, the thing was, that... I just..." Mothy couldn't finish his sentences. He couldn't bring himself to start.

"Mothy... listen. You don't have to talk about it if you aren't ready. I want to know, don't get me wrong. But if it's too much, I'm happy to just leave it."

"But you'll be working for months on the ship. I thought all of this was to get out of a punishment."

"Initially... yes. Yes, it was. But that's passed. The sun was setting when we came down here. The Captain and Ungul have probably already spoken and there's no point going now."

"She told you my middle name before you followed me, though. You could have spoken to him first and then to me."

"Yes... but that wouldn't have meant as much to you. Am I right?"

Mothy laughed. "Actually, it wouldn't have phased me in the slightest. It may have been a better option because then we would spend more time together after you finished that one week of work."

Wolflock's face dropped sourly.

"Why do you do this to me?"

Mothy shrugged. "You're the smart one. You tell me. Alright. I'm ready. I'll tell you about the Meldryk's slave mill."

CHAPTER 9

The Price of Freedom

Slaves aren't branded at birth," Mothy began. "If one was born to a slave mother, then they wait until the child is sure to survive before marking them.

"My Ma's name was Meithrin. She gave birth to me alone on the barn floor amongst the sheep and pigs."

Wolflock could only imagine the filthy smells and fluids mixed with her own. She probably had known she'd get some kind of infection.

"Ma said to me, as I was quieted by her breast, she carried me to the river. The birth had been easy, and it overjoyed her to see I was alive. She said my cry was strong and my body felt fit. She smiled to herself as she bathed in the cool river water, thinking about how much food the cook had stolen for her. The entire house staff had helped her through the pregnancy and they all knew it was the Master's doing. He had forced himself on her so regularly that it couldn't have been anyone else.

"Meithrin had taken to hiding with the animals and the other servants knew to warn her about the Master's approach. The Lady of the house ignored their complaints and protested that her husband would never do such a thing.

"That didn't matter then, though.

"She enjoyed the most perfect moment with me. She said I was the most perfect child. She always liked describing it. The sun glittering over the river as it split the horizon and all the moths flittering through the wildflowers in the meadows beyond.

"'My son shall be free,' she breathed to herself. 'My son is free. My son... is Mothy.'

"The Lord and Lady did not find out about me until I was six moons old. I was told all the time that I was a bright lad, always laughing and smiling, wanting to touch and play with everything my chubby little hands could reach. I was such an adorable baby that everyone gushed over me, especially the old cook.

"Charin, the cook, told me every time she saw me that I'd been blessed by the Goddess of Fortune, Lokkich. The old cuddly cook loved to tell me all the stories of the gods, but my favourite was of the Sun God, Shallin, who shot their golden arrows to the Earth's flowers to help them grow and blessed certain flowers with the magic to heal.

"I loved that the weeds growing around the estate that was so overlooked could be so powerful. Ma said I learned to crawl faster than the other slave children, and I remember getting into trouble for running away, laughing, as my mother chased after me. When I was older, my Ma taught all the children to read as she'd been moved to nursemaid and nanny when the Lady of the house had given birth to a little girl. I didn't understand what was going on most of the time, but Ma always encouraged me to play the 'sneaky shadows' game. Whenever the masters were about, we had to be 'sneaky shadows' and creep about without making a peep. If they caught you you had to stand as still as stone, pretending to be invisible." He chuckled at the nostalgic memory.

"I never saw work as work. I always had to make a

game out of even the most mundane chores. The younger children all had more fun when they worked with me and it made the estate a happy place to live. Even for a slave."

His eyes and smile dropped, and he stared just beyond his shoes, not making eye contact with Wolflock.

"That was until the Master's family came to stay.

"I was only six Springs old when I saw the carriages and cart rolling down the road towards the manor house. I'd excitedly run back through the fields to see who had come to visit and if they'd brought any new animals for the barn. At first, I thought they had brought some strange sickly looking creatures and then I realised the carts were all drawn by slaves. It was horrible. Their matted, filthy hair-covered bodies looked like skeletons. They wore nothing more than grimy rags and there was no sparkle in their eyes. Some were in carts topped with cages, sitting silently and staring at the ground. Many had tattoos, piercings or burn marks on their leathery skin. None smiled. None sang. They stank of death and decay."

Wolflock tried to stay impartial, but the agony seeping from his friend was hard to bear and his face filled with concern and sympathy.

"I ran back to Ma. She said I looked pale.

"That night the Master's new family held a great feast. They were all fat, pale, and balding old men with wives shrouded in black who looked as if they had poo under their noses.

"I snuck into the rafters and watched them as I always did when Ma had other chores to do. The fattest man stood next to the Master and clapped him on the shoulder, making a toast with an overflowing goblet.

"'My family! We, who have been persecuted, tormented and held in the lowest pits of disdain, finally find our true home. Our brother here has offered us his estate to begin building our paradise! Once again, we can rise to our former glory!'

"The men gave a single loud chant, '*Ahlwanye!*'

"'After they drove us from our homes through the injustice of those who would dare defy the great Trost, we endured!'

"'*Ahlwanye!*'

"'After fleeing the persecution of those who would strip the one true God of His right to rule over all! After feeling the sting of their intolerance yet again! We survived!'

"'*Ahlwanye!*'

"'And our gracious brother has brought us into his home with open arms and an open heart, saving us from an unrighteous end!'

"'*Ahlwanye*!'

"'We shall rebuild! We shall be born again and make this the haven of our Lord! The almighty Trost shall rest his eyes upon us and he shall smile! Our power restored, our women bred and all others subservient to the one and only true God!'

"'*Ahlwanye! Ahlwanye! Ahlwanye*!'

"I didn't know what they were shouting, but I remember having to stifle a laugh with my fist thinking of how such a fat man could run from anyone. I slipped out of the rafters unnoticed and found my Ma sleeping in the barn. Nestling up with her for the night, I didn't realise how much I should have relished that final evening of peace.

"The next morning was grey and dreary. The Master had all the slaves line up by a huge bonfire in the field. I didn't realise what they were burning at first. Then I saw the cover of one of the Lady of the house's favourite books. They were burning her entire library, shelves and all.

"'What have they done, mama?' I remember

crying into Ma's skirt.

"'I don't know, Mothy. Stay by me. I'll keep you safe.'

"It was the only time she'd ever broken a promise to me.

"The fat man I saw giving speeches the night before walked forward, his four chins jiggling as he moved up and down the line. The slaves he brought were standing to the sides like thin sickly trees.

"'In the beginning, the great Trost made all we see. It has not changed for hundreds of years. He, in his glory, made men to be his faithful servants, but man had so many other menial things to do that he could not spend his days in worship of the great Trost. For this he made women. Women also served to bear her man children. They took daughters to build friendships with man's friends and to bare more children. They took sons to serve the great Trost. But all men are flawed. They listened to women talk of their 'mother magic,' he spat savagely. 'Women took men away from their true purpose and the great Trost took insult to this! He struck down disease unto the land, stripping its bounty as a reprimand for woman's lies! Only those who give themselves entirely over to the great Trost shall be saved on judgement day! Only those who renounce their shameless lies of magic and other gods shall stand a chance of being embraced by the great Trost when they die!'

"He brandished a long iron pole along the line of us before leaving it in the bonfire behind him.

"'I give you this chance now. Save your souls! Save yourself an eternity of pain and suffering. Accept the mark of Trost unto your impure flesh and shine with his glory!'

"The slaves looked anxiously to one another and shrugged. They had no idea what he was talking about and no idea what he wanted them to do.

"'Heathen scum!' he spat again. He was very fond of spitting everywhere and on everything. 'As lesser beings that crawl amongst the animals and filth, they have no true word in this. Brother, I am sorry, but your house is one of sin! It must be cleansed and thank Trost we are here to help destroy the demons of temptation for you. We shall purify this land and build Trost's land to its full glory! Bring forward that farmhand.'

"Of any days in my life, two stand out among all others. I remember every single detail of this day. I remember Bergy, a slender lad of fourteen, who was yanked forward by two of the leathery slaves and they lifted his shirt up. I just remember the fear and confusion in the older boy's face. I remember the sizzling noise and the screams.

Each of the forty-two slaves was hauled forward, regardless of age or infirmity, and branded with the hot iron. Charin held me as they seared Ma on her back. It's strange how the tears that streamed down her face cleaned her skin..."

Mothy stopped for a moment, swallowing and not blinking. It was if he didn't want to close his eyes for fear of seeing the images with more clarity.

"'Why are they hurting her? They have to stop! They're hurting everyone!' I cried to Charin. Her stone face held strong for them all, but I was so confused.

"Then they reached for me.

"Ma screamed, coming to her senses and racing forward to cover me. 'No, please! Please! He'll convert! Please!'

"But there was no mercy.

"As I screamed in anguish when the red-hot iron blazed against my back, the fat man cheered about how pleased Trost would be at my pain. How a child of six deserved punishment for his sins. How he was now purified of all his wrongdoings.

"Ma wept as she held me and, not a moment later, I was unconscious. I heard later that Charin, our surly cook, stepped forward and snatched the hot iron off the man in black.

"'If it's to be done, it'll be done by me!' she snarled like a bear Ma said.

"Charin gritted her teeth and pressed the blazing iron to her rear, making no noise at all and staring down the fat man. Finally, she pulled it away, spat and limped back to the line.

"'Now, every time I take a shit, Trost can smell it.'

"I heard what had happened from Charin later when I was helping her put ointment and poultices on the burned slaves. It was weeks later that I found out how savagely she'd been beaten for that remark." Mothy stopped again, shame washing over his face in the dimming fairy dust light.

"I... I don't feel ready to talk about the details of what life was like for those years. I think it was five years they were there. Everything just got worse. They had someone guarding the kitchens and measuring all the food, so it was hard to steal. We all starved. We were all beaten. I'd never had to lie so much in my entire life. If they caught you lying, or even thought you were trying to deceive them, they'd hit you. I learned to keep my hand up to block their hits when I lie. I have a scar by my ear from where I was hit with a wineglass for just trying to be nice to one of them. I was trying to see if being their friend could get us some kindness..."

"We often got sick because we couldn't clean our living space and we weren't given medicine. We weren't given new clothes, so any that worked outside had to do it naked if their clothes rotted off. It was horrible... yet Ma was always a light in the darkness. She still sang, she still taught the children. She kept us safe, took on our workload, stole food for us and always offered to take any punishments. I'd go out at night and try to find more food and steal clean water from the water tank. I got found out, and they left Berger in the tank until he drowned, and his body poisoned the water. We had to live with that kind of thing for five years... It didn't matter how many slaves died, they always had new ones coming in. I don't know where they got them from and the new ones never spoke.

"One day I saw the Master beat his daughter at the urging of the fat man. We started calling him Loud Pockets because we imagined he used his chins as pockets. Anyway," Mothy waved his hand with a chuckle.

"I went up to the girl and comforted her. I couldn't be mean to her. She was so quiet all the time and she was treated no better than us. We became friends, and she helped us. She asked for seconds and would bring us food. She helped us sew our clothes back together and even helped me steal medicine when Ma got sick."

"What was her name?" Wolflock asked with a smile, hoping that some good came to his friend out of his kindness.

"Verrader."

"Wait... if she was Master Meldryk's daughter-"

"No. Don't say it. Not listening!" Mothy put his hands over his ears and pulled silly faces at Wolflock to silence him. "I thought that too. I thought that if we... that if the Master was our..." he swallowed as if he had just eaten something foul, "... sire... then we could be friends. Maybe we could be a family. She did what she could do for us, but I found out later it was all a game to her. A bit of rebellious cheek.

"Ma was still teaching everyone to read and write, but, with the books all burnt except for their sacred text, it was hard, so we made up a language. We taught it to Verrader too, so we could communicate in secret."

Mothy's face darkened again.

"Then... they killed Charin. She spoke back one too many times. She defied them too proudly. I'd been dreaming of running away for years at this stage but, when they killed the old cook on the stake for being a witch... just because she hung some rosemary at the door to keep the bugs away... She didn't scream though. She coughed and shrieked all damnation on them, but not once did she make a noise in pain.

"I felt so guilty that I hadn't gotten everyone to escape beforehand that I brought our plans forward. We grabbed what we could and tried to sneak away. I asked Verrader for help. I trusted her.

"I shouldn't have.

"We had to kill one guard on the way out. Verrader was meant to make a scene in her room and call everyone to her. We joked about her pretending to be possessed by a demon and I thought she'd done it. Just before we got into the forest, all the Trostons appeared in front of us. It was mayhem. We scattered and ran, but if we weren't caught, we were killed on the spot. All my friends. All the kids I grew up with. All the remaining free-thinking slaves..."

Wolflock wanted to ask him to stop. It was too much. His gut clenched and Mothy's shaking hurt his heart.

"Of course, Verrader had told them everything, even telling them our secret code. They kept us locked up that night, and we knew something terrible was going to happen because they didn't beat us. "Verrader came to where we were locked up. She tried to explain that she was in love with me and that she couldn't let us leave. I was so angry, I couldn't speak. The next morning, they pulled all the slaves to the forest, where we nearly escaped. For hours they tortured everyone, Loud Pockets screaming how we'd betrayed them and the Lord. To stop another escape attempt, they slaughtered everyone. Verrader begged them not to hurt me. I wish they had. They'd read the notes and knew I was the one who organised and led everyone. They were going to make an example of me.

They burnt... they killed Ma in front of me. They chained me to a tree, put hot coals at my feet and said I'd starve to death before anyone helped me. No one but them knew I was there."

"How on earth did you survive?" Wolflock breathed, squeezing Mothy's arm to support him.

"I believe Ma's spirit cared for me over that next week. I ate the bugs that crawled on me and it rained every afternoon. Eight days later, I saw billows of smoke rising from the Master's land."

"That was when they were discovered for harbouring the Talons saboteur. The man who plotted to kill the king," Wolflock interjected.

"That's when the name Meldryk didn't just mean 'from the powerful mill' anymore. That's when all of Puinteyle found out that the Meldryk's were a mill for slaves."

"That's why you don't want the name anymore."

"Exactly. Who wants to be associated with the thing that killed my Ma? Anyway, no one found me. I was really hopeful too, but no one came. I barely made it, but, one morning, I woke up and the chains were a bit loose. I wriggled and wriggled until I was free. I didn't know if anyone at the house was still alive, so I went in the opposite direction following the tree line. I found a river and followed that too.

"After days of wandering with blistered feet and only the call of bugs to eat driving me on, I stumbled across the road. I just kept going until I collapsed from exhaustion.

"But old Charin was right. The goddess of fortune had blessed me, because only an hour later did a merchant find me. The nomadic man didn't hesitate to check me over and give me all the food and water he could. Hazzim was the strangest man I'd had ever seen and the first person not in rags to treat me with any kindness.

"His hair was as black as night and the strands were so thick that his long plait looked like a satin rope. His skin was naturally olive and his huge hooked nose made him look like a parrot. His warm brown eyes had not only been filled with kindness, but he had also been honest. He had me travel with him to Shellinden and told me with stories of the world and his travels. It took us nearly a month, but in that time, we became good friends.

"Hazzim taught me once again that the world was good at its core. He reinforced Ma's lessons of all the wonder in the world and how beautiful life could be. He was patient with my initial mood swings and terror whenever he lit a fire or we came across a Troston symbol. He also said I went pale at the sounds of chains, so Hazzim made sure no metal made noise around me. Hazzim showed me the joys of good fabrics and how dressing up and staying clean left one feeling proud and powerful. He also taught me how amazing food is. With Hazzim's spice and knick-knacks cart, I saw hundreds of trades with food stalls. My stomach would grumble and pick out something tasty like exotic fruits, cakes and legs of meat. Hazzim would smile and ask them to throw in whatever it was I was eyeing. That night we would cook it up, sing and dance with whatever friends we had made in the day.

"'Good food brings people together, Mothy, my boy! As do good hearts!'

"I just smiled, but I didn't understand. Hazzim just trusted I would pick up the lessons one day.

"When we finally reached Shellinden, Hazzim fell ill. We were staying at an inn by the docks and Hazzim sent me out to get medicine. I had been so afraid of being beaten for asking for help for my friend that I just hopped from foot to foot, hoping to see the right herb growing out of a crack in the path.

"A young lady with sun-streaked brown hair came to my aid, seeing my distress and asked me if everything was well. She had such a soft and kind face. I told her all about Hazzim and she smiled wisely. Her name was Mira Flore, and she was the local doctor. She came to Hazzim's aid and checked on us both daily. To prevent me from catching the same illness, she asked if I would like to help her with the community gardens and come with her to the university one day. I was so excited to go and Hazzim said it would be best to just let him sleep away the sickness.

"For the first time, I saw how the world really was.

"The world was colourful, kind and compassionate.

"I accidentally knocked over a pot plant on my first day helping Mira and shattered the pot. I had instantly jumped away and flinched, expecting to be beaten, but she just laughed and got me to glue the pieces back together.

"'When people cause harm and it is an accident, they just need to do everything in their power to help others recover from it. That is how a good community works!'

"'But I'm a disgusting and horrible insect for breaking it...' I said, shaking. It's what I'd heard for far lesser offences.

"'Did you do it on purpose?'

"'No...'

"'Then you're still delightful and funny, and I still enjoy your company.'

"'What if you thought it was on purpose though?'

"'Me personally? Well then, I would think

that you had some other things that were hurting you. Perhaps you want some more attention and don't know how to ask for it. Maybe you're mad and don't know how to express it safely. Maybe you just really hated that pot!'

"I sat in silence and thought hard on what she'd said, holding two pieces together.

"'What if I couldn't fix it? Like, if I had no hands!'

"'Then you'd have to buy me a new one or something of what I thought had equal value.'

"'And if I didn't have any money?'

"'Then we'd have to sit down and work it out so that we both felt better.'

"'And what if I didn't want to talk?'

"'Well, you had caused me some pain. If you were very stubborn still, I would speak to the local Guards and they would sit us both down until we both felt like we had reached a better solution.'

"'And if they can't find a solution?'

"'They don't stop until they do.'

"'That must be frustrating.'

"'I'm sure it would be, but they are specially trained for these issues. This way, both people eventually walk away happy and the community as a whole feels safer and more loving.'

"'So, the Guards are good people?'

"Mira just laughed 'Yes, darling. Yes, they are. As are you and I. We all look after each other as we should. That's why I asked you if you were well. You looked so upset and I had a feeling I could help.'

"Each day, after that, I spent long hours with Mira and, eventually, she took me to the University of Shellinden. It was the largest arts and history university ever known. I was entranced by the students rushing back and forth, the lecturers in their halls, the beauty and the knowledge... Mira said my love for it was palpable.

"She encouraged me, letting me speak to whoever I wanted to and helped me ask the questions I couldn't quite think of.

"I asked her one day if she'd studied here when we left with baskets of herbs from the small medicinal garden.

"'The medical faculty here is fairly small. I travelled all the way to Mystentine to study medicine. That's where the best doctors are trained,' Mira smiled proudly.

"When Mira showed me the map of Puinteyle, it overwhelmed me. The world was so big! She showed me the vast distance she had to travel to get there from

Shellinden.

"'The journey was so far that I nearly chose not to make it. But it is where the best doctors are trained, and I wanted to help heal people as best I could.'

"'Do you think I could study there?' I asked her.

"Mira just hugged me and gave me a dandelion flower from the basket.

"'Do you know what this flower is?' she asked gently, looking me right in the eye.

"'A weed?'

"'Yes. But it's also a lion's face. This little flower helps people with bad organs. It soaks deeply into their bodies and heals them powerfully. But it has to be taken daily for many. If you work hard and be like the dandelion, you can heal even the most stubborn diseases.'

"'But you said it's a weed.'

"'It is. This funny little flower will grow wherever you plant it. It will grow wherever it likes. It will find a crack in the path and grow there even if fifty people trample it every day. It will keep growing and showing its beautiful lion's face because it has a bigger purpose. It has a bigger mission in life.'

"The way she speaks is enchanting. I held the

flower and smiled hopefully. 'What does that mean?'

"'Be the dandelion. Be bright. Bring happiness. Heal deeply. If you work every day and grow wherever you want to grow, even if fifty people try to trample you every day, then you'll have the blessing of the dandelion.'

"I felt as if Mira had lit a sun inside of my heart. I was hearing Ma through Mira. I decided then and there that I was going to study at Mystentine one day and be a dandelion.

"Mira cared for me and Hazzim until he was back to full health. I expected to leave and continue travelling (hopefully towards Mystentine), but Hazzim decided to set up a store by the docks. He had grown quite fond of Mira and she had developed an attachment to us both. I helped Hazzim run his new store and saved up all of my wages. I always tried to go above and beyond for my friends and made lots of new ones at the docks, including the crew of the Silver Ice Hair, who were just as playful and fun as me. I became pretty well known throughout the Shellinden docks and Hazzim's business grew. Everything was going well, and I even had counselling to help stop the night terrors of what had happened to me. It was all going pretty well... but then I saw her."

"Verrader." Wolflock answered for him.

"It was only a moment, but she was walking in between two robed men and walking behind another man dressed in black and red. Ungul stopped me from attacking her. I feel like I would have killed her there and then. Right there in that crowded street. Just her being there was enough to ruin my peace. Ungul stopped me and told Hazzim everything. I locked myself in my room but every night I'd sneak out and try to find her. I felt possessed. Mira caught me one night and talked me down. Hazzim joined in, and we organised for me to take passage on the Silver Ice Hair and get to Mystentine. Then everything happened as the others probably told you."

"Do you still want revenge?" Wolflock's eyebrows were deeply creased with concern.

"When I don't see her and I don't have the risk of seeing her, I honestly don't even think about it. It's just if she's there."

"Is that why you avoided the Troston priest? Did you think you'd hurt him too?"

"Nah." Mothy waved and chuckled. "They just give me the creeps."

Both boys broke out into belly laughs with a much-needed break in the tension.

"You knew that opening up to me would work, didn't you?"

"I knew it would clear the air." He paused for a moment. "Yes. I knew telling you about my past would make you feel a bit warmer and able to tell me about your past."

"You're right, you know?" Mothy leaned back against the wall of the box as he closed his eyes.

"I normally am. What about in particular this time?"

"It does feel terrible. But it also feels... more free."

"I won't say a word to anyone. Your secret is safe with me."

Mothy's shoulders relaxed and his soft smile reached his eyes. "Thank you, Lockie. But what are you going to tell Ungul to get out of your punishment?"

Wolflock's mouth stretched into a conceding grimace. "I won't be saying anything to her. I'll take the work."

"Really? You'd do that for me?" Mothy breathed, his eyes sparkling.

"Of course. You're the most fascinating, kind and loyal friend I've ever had and I value your love more than I will complain about some hard labour. Of course, if you want to help me with that work, I'd be much obliged, but it's not a condition or anyth-"

Wolflock stopped as Mothy launched himself forward, wrapping his arms around Wolflock's neck and hugged him so tightly, he was worried his collarbone may snap.

"I've never had a friend like you, either."

Wolflock smiled with a sigh and hugged his dear friend back.

Rhiannon D. Elton

CHAPTER 10

Handing It In

The boys went to the very end of dinner. Most of the other passengers had finished their meals and Grogen was whistling to himself as he massaged his swollen ankle. Geagle scrubbed away at the dirty dishes. The captain was grinning, leaning on the bench and sipping a mug of tea.

"Grogen! What happened?" Mothy asked as Wolflock took up the plates of vegetables and fish that had been set on the oven for them.

"He fell off the table," Geagle snorted as he scrubbed away.

"Ah yeh... go blow the other one," Grogen bantered. "Was jus' tryin' ta spice up the evenin'."

"You were dancing, Grogen?" Wolflock asked.

"Like the prettiest ballerina I ever saw!" Geagle cut in, scrubbing the top of Grogen's head with the brush.

"You're jus' salty 'cause I got outta dishes."

"Yes, yes," Captain Blutro sighed, shaking his head. "Grogen's performance was magnificent."

The boys laughed and Mothy gathered two cups and a jug of juice. Wolflock turned to the Captain, but he held up his hand.

"After my tea, lad. Go have your dinner."

Nodding, Wolflock joined Mothy, and they ate. He felt his guts winding with nerves, but at the same time, there was a sense of excitement that he knew more about Mothy than anyone else. Both boys joked about how Grogen would have danced and what they'd like to do when they were bored tomorrow.

"I want to try riding planks of wood off the back of the ship."

"We could set up a flying line from the crow's nest to the dining hall."

"It was kind of fun to jump into the sails. It might be better with a rope round your middle."

"Oh! What if we lowered each other down over the side of the ship with a bucket to catch fish?"

"Brilliant!"

Their plans became increasingly absurd and their laughter was infectious. Wolflock couldn't help but feel watched. He glanced around to see Ungul, but every time he looked at her, she was looking directly away from him.

Wolflock finished his food and followed the Captain out onto the dark deck.

"Captain Blutro?"

"Yes, Mr Felen?"

"I believe Ungul spoke to you already about my-"

"Ah yes. I understand that a week would be suitable to make amends for any ill feelings. I know you may want to contest the matter but that is my final word."

"A week?" Wolflock blinked and glanced around, expecting the Captain to say it was a joke.

"Yes, yes. I know it's a long while, but I have all faith that you will be able to write the crews' letters amicably. I'll have you write up the schedule for them as well."

"Writing letters?"

"Unless you'd like me to change your duties. I could have you making dinners or hauling barrels."

"N-no, sir! Writing letters is fine. Thank you, Captain."

"Off you go then. I have a ship to sail."

Wolflock nodded and dashed away, thinking to move back into the dining hall to tell Mothy the good news, but a solitary dark figure at the stern caught his eye.

"Ungul?"

The great woman turned to him and smiled with her mouth closed.

"Where is Uhnha?"

"At dinner."

"And you're out here?"

"I needed the fresh air. Our houses back home are more open and airier than the ones I have seen."

Wolflock hummed in agreement, not quite knowing what to say.

"No one ever speaks to me the way you did." She didn't look at him as she spoke. "I am the daughter of great leaders and descended from royalty. No person has ever bested me in combat since my coming of age. Yet you had the courage to speak to me as you did. You are very brave."

"I'm just glad you didn't say stupid," he chuckled.

"Family is everything to my people. We go through

raging rivers and blazing caverns for them. You told me the truth that I did not want to hear. That for everything I would do in action for my sister, it was my words and my heart that meant more to her. When we get home, I will help her heal and I will do as you do for your sister. I'll support her in the decisions she needs to make on her own journey."

"Aye... my family isn't that good at communicating either, to be honest. We try, though. If you keep trying to get better, then that's what counts."

They both nodded and stood in silence for a time longer, watching the tiny glints of blue fireflies glittered on the water. Unlike the fireflies that lived in the South and needed warm wet conditions, beginning as blue glow worms and becoming yellow fireflies, the Northern fireflies began as yellow ones burrowed into tree bark and then became blue ones that hunted larvae in the river water.

"Thank you, by the way."

Ungul looked at him with a sideways glance and opened her mouth to speak.

"The maramuti! The maramuti! Maramuti at the bow!" Groger howled from the crow's nest.

The Captain stomped and rang the bell by the

helm, calling the crew and company to the deck. There was a great rush as everyone on the ship raced to the top deck and hung with bated breath on the edges.

"There! I see it! I see it mama!" Tinni squealed with excitement from the starboard side as streaks of bioluminescence darted behind the branches and leaves.

Frustrated with being on the wrong side, Wolflock glanced around, turning and catching Mothy's glittering eye. They grinned together as they shared the same thought. They raced up the rigging to the crow's nest, scrambling side by side, not caring if the crew caught them. Mothy quickly pulled ahead of Wolflock and hauled him into the crow's nest, startling Groger.

"What the-!"

"Evenin' Groger," Mothy chuckled.

"Have you seen maramuti before, Groger?" Wolflock asked, leaning as far out over the edge as he could. "I've only read about them in my family's library but I'm sure pictures don't do them justice."

"There's another one!" Veluse cried out.

Wolflock and Mothy saw, through the branches, a creature with a long swirling tail lined with blue light. The end was curling and flicking like a worm.

"That's a female," Wolflock nudged Mothy. "See?

The tail is thin and whip-like. They use it to catch fish."

"And their babies when they fall out of the tree," Groger laughed.

"There's another!" Mothy jumped forward so excitedly, Wolflock had to catch him by the shirt.

The one he'd seen had a glowing little baby on her back. The long gangly legs and small flat face came into light as another dashed in front of her. She resembled a lemur with the squashed face and her baby was simply a smaller, fluffier version of its mother. Another was sitting on a tree root digging up mud crabs with a stick.

"Look!" Slavidus yelled and pointed to a pair of males playfully swinging, trying to show off to the other females. Their tails were large flat pads and the lights forked out like leaf veins.

"The flat tails are used to build huts. The better the mud hut, the more attractive they are to female maramuti," Wolflock laughed as another pair chased each other around the branches.

One of them swung too hard, and the branch cracked, breaking and dropping him into the slow waters. Only his pride was wounded as he retreated into the forest. Wolflock noticed hundreds of golden and blue sparkles glittering between the trees. The boys stopped laughing as fireflies began lifting out of the trees and bushes, raining stars all around them. The sky, the water and everything in between was adorned with the magic of the little lights.

"It's a week before Mabon," Wolflock noted, leaning back and thinking of what it meant. A time of gratitude for everything the year has brought. "It'll be a week before the fireflies and fairies reach the river by Plugh as they migrate past Corl."

"Fairies?" Mothy asked as he sat nimbly on the side of the wooden bucket.

"Just wait and see. I'm sure they'll come."

Wolflock looked down to see Tinni and the two youngest Xiayahn children dancing merrily through the mist of lights. They twirled and sang with several of the adults, overjoyed with the sight as several maramuti plopped curiously onto the deck. They began to copy the children and chase after the glowing bugs, swatting them around, but not eating them. Some of them in the tree branches began to sing a low soft "hroo" noise.

"Lockie! Look!"

Wolflock followed his gaze and saw a larger, faster figure. It zoomed back and forth between the trees, then across the water, skipping along like a dancer. Only a hand high, the glowing body of the fairy was beautiful. It spiraled around the mast and Wolflock caught a glimpse of the transparent butterfly wings as it shot off behind them.

Another fairy zoomed around, and then another. Some sat on the sails, the tips of the mast, even the people, sprinkling the entire ship in beautiful glowing dust. Some of the tiny fairies drifted daintily around the ship while others danced like little ballerinas.

Watching the mesmerising scene, Wolflock felt like he had unearthed an even greater hunger to see the world. He had always had a thirst for knowledge, but this left him wanting more in experiences. Mystentine University was his start, but who knew where his next adventure would be.

More of the fairies and fireflies travelled along the deck and Groger kicked the boys out of the crow's nest. Mothy danced with the children and made them laugh by trying to copy the fairies' dances. Wolflock saw Ungul still standing alone and went to stand by her.

"I might get to see more of these things while working for the ship," he smiled and nodded out to the deck, resigning himself to his next week.

"Oh? You do not have to do that. I did not speak

to Captain Blutro. I believe everything has been settled quite well."

"Wait... so you haven't spoken to the Captain at all?"

"No. If he asks, I'll say you don't need any jobs to do as punishment. I think you've learned your lesson."

"But. He. Wait. What!?"

Dear Mama,

Since I arrived here nearly ten days ago rather quite it...

I have become on to our other meet friend, Mothy, after I do them on mandant...

...

Your obedient Brother,

Wulfric F. Felen

About the Author

Rhiannon is the walker between worlds. One foot in Earth, the other constantly stepping into Pelaia. As if gazing into a crystal ball, she sees this other world and all that happens within it with the clarity of someone staring through a veil. It is her purpose in life to transcribe these histories, adventures and mysteries for you to enjoy.

This witchy woman was raised by a fairy who taught her that there are all kinds of magic throughout the world. She taught Rhiannon to withhold judgement because you never truly know another's story. She also taught her that everyone, no matter how flawed, has something to give.

The adventures of Rhiannon's youth lead her through trials and dangers that taught her about the darkness within the world, but it also showed her that anything could be overcome. There was always a way. Surrounded by so much apathy and hopelessness, Rhiannon made it her goal in life to show others the light and that if they could dream it they could do it.

The way she was shown this was through stories.

Stories of friendship, love, adventure, discovery, compassion, understanding, and kindness. All of these stories gave her new friends, new lessons, new life.

In the depths of her darkest place during year 11 and 12, when she felt at her loneliest, drugs surrounded her life in terrible ways, the self worth of those she loved and admired crumbled, she was relentlessly bullied and felt friendless in her most trying years, she lived in squalor due to bureaucratic errors, and yet she still had to be "perfect". She had to perfectly excel in school, she had to perfectly remain calm and gentle in the face of abusive men, she had to be a perfect role model for all those around her. That craving for perfection in order to get love nearly killed her several times. In all of this darkness with politicians sacrificing real people and real environments for imaginary money, with teachers displaying no compassion for their students, with men abusing women and children, with communities vilifying those who needed them most, with injustice reigning and all hope seemingly lost... Puinteyle was born.

All of these pains in life were fixed in Puinteyle.

All of them were able to be mended and healed because of a conscientious effort. The people of Puinteyle wanted to be better than their problems. Puinteyle was where people made an effort to love freely and always sought to help each other, animals and the environment. Harmony. True and beautiful harmony. Where the pendulum never swayed too far away from that beautiful harmonious and happy point of balance.

But like in our lives, there is always obstacles to overcome and darkness to understand. Therefore, Puinteyle would always have its own inner turmoils to learn and grow from too. Thus, the stories never truly end.

Rhiannon has always lived and breathed stories, knowing her role in life is to be this guide through a new world for others. Her dream is to support her community with her stories, as well as creating a company where other artists can come together in celebration of Pelaia and all it has to offer.

Get More of the Magic & Mystery...

subscribe.rhiannoneltonauthor.com/more

If you want more clues, more magic and more mystery, let me know by going to the Case of Mothy's subscribe page.

You'll get clues, maps, sketches, behind the scenes stories, lore and much more! You'll also be the first to know when a new story is coming out so you can solve the mystery before your friends.

If you sign up with the magical link below, you'll also get a free downloadable map to follow Wolflock's journey to Mystentine University.

subscribe.rhiannoneltonauthor.com/more

Thank you for being part of the magic and mystery. By supporting an independently published Australian author you make sure that more of the story can be told. Australia's independent authors need the support of their local community to continue to produce the books we all love.

If you enjoyed this book, please leave a positive review online (where you purchased the book or on Goodreads), recommend this book to your friends or family, or purchase another copy to gift to a loved one.

Stay tuned for the next mystery in the series:

THE WOLFLOCK CASES

BOOK 3

THE CASE OF THE CURSE OF HOUL

www.rhiannoneltonauthor.com

 RhiDElton

 RhiannonEltonAuthor

 RhiDElton

 rhiannoneltonauthor

 Rhiannon D. Elton

 RhiDElton

THE WOLFLOCK CASES

1. The Case of the Captain's Hair - Now Available

2. The Case of Mothy - Now Available

3. The Case of the Curse of Houl - Now Available

4. The Case of the Bitter Draught – Now Available

5. The Study in Silver - December 2020

6. The Case of the Lost Mermaid - March 2021

7. The Case of the Pisces Moon - May 2021

8. The Case of the Haemophageous Equine - July 2021

9. The Case of the Lost Antrum - September 2021

10. The Case of the Mountain's Monster - December 2021

Dedicated to Kristel

For showing me that two oddballs can achieve great things at three in the morning. Our paths may weave closer and further from each other, but inspiration never dies.

Get More of the Magic & Mystery...

subscribe.rhiannoneltonauthor.com/more

If you want more clues, more magic and more mystery, let me know by going to the Case of Mothy's subscribe page.

You'll get clues, maps, sketches, behind the scenes stories, lore and much more! You'll also be the first to know when a new story is coming out so you can solve the mystery before your friends.

If you sign up with the magical link below, you'll also get a free downloadable map to follow Wolflock's journey to Mystentine University.

subscribe.rhiannoneltonauthor.com/more